About the author

Dael Akkerman was a lawyer and a freelance writer, illustrator and photographer. After leaving Amsterdam, she studied archaeology, anthropology, philosophy and the history of religion in New York, Paris, Naples, London and St Petersburg, before settling in England, where she spent the rest of her life.

Noema is her only novel.

NOEMA

a novel

ISBN 978-3-949666-07-0

This is a story about some things that happened to me about twelve thousand years ago.

I was very, very young then, and these are probably my earliest memories. It would help me a great deal if you were to listen, but I assure you that I'll understand completely if you don't want to. After all, you may well feel that my memories couldn't possibly be of the slightest relevance to you. But if you are prepared to listen, I hope that by the time I'm finished, you'll agree that perhaps they are.

*

Before I begin, I need first to tell you another story. One that was told to me, as it was told to everyone, as soon as we were old enough to hear it. It's very short, and it goes like this.

Before the beginning of all things, in the space before space and in the time before time, there was the All Life. The All Life did not know it was the All Life, as it was not called that, there being nothing anywhere else to call it anything. It simply was: and it was the only thing that was.

The All Life knew nothing but the fact of itself, for there was nothing else for it to know. But it could feel, and what it felt was meaninglessness of a kind never known by anything since.

Then the All Life began to grow. By the very act of growing, it created another place, a place where there was space and time, and so the All Life created space and time as well. At first, this other place, where there was space and time and which one day would be called the world, was without light, without heat and without life. And yet, into this dark and dead place, forms of the All Life began to appear. First, it appeared as what one day would be called fire, common to all living things, but which now formed first the sun and then the moon. Then it appeared as what one day would be called air, until the world, that was yet to be called the world, was filled with it. Then the light from the fire of the sun and the moon began to warm the air, until what would one day be called rain, the first rain that ever was, began to fall. After the longest time, although there was still no one to call it time, further forms of the All Life began to appear in the world as earth, then grass, trees and all other things that live in the ground. Then, when the All Life had almost filled the world with itself in these forms, it began to appear as animals, and finally, as people.

That which makes anything what it truly is—whether fire, water, earth, grass, a tree, an animal or a person—is therefore an indivisible part of the All Life. And by manifesting itself in the world in these forms, forms that in due course could, however imperfectly, be understood, the All Life fulfilled what had always been its true, although hitherto unknown purpose: to become alive. Because a thing not perceived to be alive cannot truly live at all.

*

As I say, I first heard this about twelve thousand years ago, when I was very young. In fact, now that I've had a little time to reflect on it, I can definitely say that it is indeed the earliest thing I can remember. And by the way, if it gave you a vague and slightly unsettling feeling of seeming familiar even though you know you've never seen or heard it before, please don't worry. It's because people have been telling this story to one another, or at least something like it, for a very long time.

*

I mentioned just now that you may well feel that none of what I'm proposing to tell you can be relevant to you. But if you are still listening, I need to make a few things clear before going any further. First, I have to explain why I can't begin by introducing myself. I know that this may seem like an annoying attempt to make myself appear mysterious, but in fact, it's the simple truth. Introducing oneself means giving some explanation of who one is, and I realised quite some time ago that I can only do that by actually telling you my story. But at the same time, I don't really want to be telling you a story at all. Not that I have anything against stories. Far from it. When I was growing up, stories were an essential part of life. In addition to the story that I began with, we all told one another stories to help us understand as many aspects of this world as possible. Not just about things that would either keep you alive or kill you, but stories that explained why there are so many hundreds of types of insects, or the lifecycle of the perch, or the breaking strength of rope made from nettle twine, or when nettle twine rope is better than the stronger but less wieldy rope made from heather stalks, or the importance of spotting an oak weevil when gathering acorns.

Another important element of this kind of story was its connection to a particular place that you already knew, so that when you went to that place, you would remember the story and would, for example, know exactly where on the river you could put your fish trap, or where you could find the best heather for making rope if you needed to pull a felled birch tree trunk, and things like that.

I'm so sorry, I'm digressing. What I'm trying to say is that I'd far prefer it if the two of us, you and I, could just have a conversation, the kind in which we could really find things out about one another. That would make it easier for me to explain things, such as instead of just always being here, that I came into this world like everyone else, although I did so in a time that could seem to you a very distant one indeed. I could give you a better idea of the village and the family into which I was born and who gave me the name Maya, the first name of all the thousands and thousands of names I have had since.

We could talk about what things were like just before the time I was born, how the village into which I was born had to move to a lower slope of one of the big hills above Verba, the great northern river, a hill which like almost everywhere else was completely covered in trees, mostly birch and hazel lower down, but with plenty of oak, elm and ash too, with pine higher up and with only a few number of small clearings. We'd talk about life in my village, and of course about my family: my two older twin brothers, Breccan and Rod, both usually teasing me as boys do, but always there to help look after me until I was better able to look after myself. I'd tell you about our younger sister Edra and our baby brother Bran, named for his father, but who we always called Little Bran, to avoid confusion. We'd talk about my mother Frey and my father, Bran, their friend Serris, and about Serris' daughter Arlen, who was my best friend, to whom I owe everything and without whom I doubt I'd be telling you this story now. We would talk about the person we all called the Traveller: and, although even now I find the subject difficult, we would have to talk about the mysterious people known only as the Lost Ones.

When I say that we could talk about all these things in a conversation, I mean that if I said something you didn't understand, or was telling you something you already knew, you could say so, and we could deal with any little difficulty right then and there. Not that I'm saying that we'd deal with it satisfactorily, mind you. There have been many times when some misunderstanding or other has led to the conversation in question ending rather badly. I'll probably have to return to that subject a little later, but the point I'm trying to make now is that having that kind of conversation or discussion or whatever you want to call it seems to be increasingly difficult these days. I have my own ideas as to why that should be, but for now, I suppose I just have to accept that's how it is and that all I can do is tell you the story of what happened to me and to those I knew in that different time.

However, the fact that it's a story almost entirely about me is another reason I'm taking this long actually to begin it. In the time I'm going to tell you about, talking about yourself without being invited to do so was basically seen as boasting, which was always considered to be in very poor taste. Also, telling a story about oneself ought presumably to start with an explanation of who one is, and as I said just now, I can't do that yet. In fact, I now find the subject more bewildering than ever, to the point where the mere prospect of attempting to explain who I am confuses me so much that I tend completely to forget what I was saying. Which is of course precisely what has now happened.

Where was I? Oh yes. I was trying to tell you about the things that we need to try and get clear.

The next thing is the fact that you and I know a lot less about one another than you might have assumed. I know so many people who are convinced not just that I already know everything about them, but that they know everything about me. Perhaps I should be used to this by now, but I still find that kind of certainty both naïve and a little disturbing. Worse still, a lot of these people can get terribly upset when they finally realise how wrong they are. In fact, some of them get so upset that they end up blaming me and, in some cases, resenting or even hating me. So I want to be as clear about this as I can be right from the very beginning in the hope that you don't end up doing the same.

The next thing I need to explain is a lot more difficult.

I've already mentioned that it may well seem to you that nearly everything I'm going to tell you about happened a very long time ago. But I'm going to ask you to try and disregard that completely. My reason for asking this is that this is, quite simply, not the way I have ever seen time, and so it isn't the basis on which I can tell you this story.

You see, you probably view the past and the future as things at different points on a single line called Time. But when I was younger, we didn't see the past and the future like that at all, but merely as different parts of our world. Getting to them might be difficult, but that didn't stop them from being parts of the world any more than, say, a particular river wasn't a part of the world just because it happened to be three valleys away and getting to it took a lot of effort.

In saying this, I'm not trying to imply that the way you see the past and the future is wrong, merely that it can create certain difficulties. When you put both the past and the future on one long line called Time, you can only look for things in them up or down that line, which is rather limiting, particularly when you're trying to look for something in the past. First, the further away something is, the harder it is to judge distance. We accept this when we look at something over a distance in space, like a fir tree or a rock outcrop that turns out on closer inspection to be nowhere near as big as it first seemed from a long way away. But we overlook it completely when we're looking at something over a distance not in space, but in time. Something that from where we're standing looks large and therefore really important may not look nearly as large or important to the people who are living close to it. Similarly, we can look at several things that, from where we're standing, look like they're very close together, so we assume they must be connected. But someone who is actually there might see that the things in question are quite some distance from one another and therefore not connected at all.

The second difficulty with seeing the past and the future in this way is a much more serious one, certainly so far as what I'm about to tell you is concerned. I've heard it said lately that although we can shape the future, we can't change the past. I don't mean to be rude, but really, that is such nonsense. People who say this have lost sight of something that when I was young was taken for granted, which is that a memory, any memory, is something about yesterday that you happen to need today. If someone remembers something happening in a particular way, it's because they need to, and the fact that someone else might need to re-member the same thing in a totally different way is neither here nor there. Of course it's often the case that what I need to remember is exactly the same as what you need to remember, such as the quickest route to the nearest fresh water, or where to find the moss necessary to make a poultice that will stop a wound from bleeding. But more personal memories, memories bound up with strong feelings, are inevitably going to be very different, and as I said just now, if that's not understood from the outset, then very little of this story will make any sense.

Perhaps that doesn't matter. But if we lose the ability to see the past properly, we will also stop being able to see all the thousands of examples of hope replacing despair, ingenuity arising from stupidity, compassion in the face of cruelty, kindness supplanting indifference. And that seems to me to matter very much.

I don't know when people began to see different times in this very limiting way, so I don't really know why they started doing so. No doubt it's yet another manifestation of our talent for taking the minor distinctions amongst ourselves and transforming them into major differences. I realise that without this ability, we would never have been able to kill one another or allow one another to starve to death in the quantities that we have, so I am very well aware of the irony in me of all people bemoaning it. But I simply cannot understand why people fixate on differences between themselves and those with whom there can never be any question of competing, such as people who happen to live in a different time. But that is enough on that subject. All I really mean to say right now is that I don't see time as you probably do, so please don't be surprised if I get a little muddled with my tenses now and again.

One last thing. If by now you're asking yourself if it wouldn't be simpler just to say that I'm not perfect, that I make mistakes and that I don't know everything, all I can say is that I have told so many people exactly that, more times than I care to remember, and most of them, the vast majority of them in fact, flatly refuse to believe it. I have to say that I have always found it strange how people are perfectly capable of believing the most extraordinary things, like a small child one day becoming a bird, whereas if they really don't want to believe something, they won't, no matter how obviously true it may be.

But now it's time to make a proper start, as the small child turning into a bird is a very good place to do so. I say that because this is where it all really began and because the child in question used to be me.

*

Of course, I didn't actually turn into a bird.

However, I still put it like that because I was very young at the time, and it was the only way I could really describe what had happened to me. In fact, most people who learned about it guessed pretty much straight away that what actually did happen to me was not nearly so straightforward as simply turning into a bird. They realised that somehow, I hadn't just been brought into direct contact with the All Life, but that I had almost immediately returned to this world. What was particularly remarkable about this was that so far as anyone then knew—including, up to that point, myself—only the Traveller could do this.

I mentioned the Traveller a little while ago. She is in many ways a unique figure. The most obvious way in which She is unique is that no one knows or has even heard of a time when She was not simply there. It is therefore widely assumed that She always has been. In fact, some people say this is the only way that everything could possibly have come to be as it is. They say that the various manifestations of the All Life that we are capable of understanding in this world, including ourselves, are very poor representations of their true nature as aspects of the All Life: so poor, in fact, that it is quite impossible for any single such mani-festation to have any understanding of another one. Yet without some understanding, nothing in this world could ever survive, so there has to be someone who knows at least something of the true nature of all these manifestations, and who therefore can relay this knowledge to the rest of us here in this world. Someone who, in short, has access to and from the All Life. That person is the Traveller.

Yet not everyone agrees with this. Some other people say—albeit there are few such people, and they say this quietly and discreetly—that the Lost Ones may well have seen things very differently from the way we do, including the All Life. They say that if only a fraction of what is whispered about the Lost Ones is true, they could do the most extraordinary things. According to one story, they could somehow make all other animals and plants, even the trees, do their bidding. Another tells of how they all lived together in vast villages, each one hundreds of times bigger than the largest village of the kind we know. According to yet another, these vast villages were made up of huge houses, built not of wood and mud and reed but entirely of stone, and were not situated amongst trees at all but in enormous expanses of open space in which there were hardly any trees to begin with. On top of all of this, it is said that the Lost Ones somehow managed to find food enough to feed themselves so that none of them ever went hungry, let alone starved. If, say the people who repeat such stories, the Lost Ones could do all these things, perhaps they had no Traveller because they had no need of information and understanding from the All Life, whereas by contrast, we have a Traveller because our need for such information and understanding is so pressing.

But as I say, this view is not shared by many, and it is seldom expressed openly. This is because most people consider it to be in the poorest possible taste to refer to the Lost Ones at all, except in negative or cautionary terms. This in turn is because that, so far from having the wisdom that should have resulted from their great knowledge and power, the Lost Ones had only pride. Since pride without wisdom leads to arrogance, the Lost Ones became uncaring and cruel, not merely to everything else in the world, but even to one another, until their great knowledge and power was turned against them, although this was in such a distant time that no one really knows how. However it happened, the result was that they vanished from the world so completely that in the time of which I'm about to tell you, only two traces of them remain which, as I'll also explain, serve only as the direst of warnings.

In any case, again until quite recently, people usually wouldn't have the time or patience for speculation about the Lost Ones and what became of them, because it makes little difference to their lives, and because it does not seem to relate in any way to the story I told you when we began. Each village within each of the four Federations has its own version of this story, but the basic theme is always the same: how all the things in this world, everything that makes it the world, including ourselves, are merely imperfect manifestations of the many aspects of the All Life, to which somehow or other, all must return.

The variations and embellishments in each individual story lie in the details of how this, that or the other village survived the Great Cold. This is the name we give to the time, different to the time of the Lost Ones, when the All Life suddenly began to withdraw from the world. In its place, the snow and ice gathered, first in the north, then seeping further and further south, slowly filling the void that the All Life left as it withdrew until the world is left to the Great Cold. The parts that aren't ice are dry areas of land covered in dun-coloured grass, lichen and sedge with the odd clump of stunted willow, juniper or birch clinging onto small patches of earth left in the crevices of the rock, salty through the lack of rain, covered in snow in winter and blasted by frigid, dust-laden wind in the summer. The animals are reduced to some scrawny lemmings and a few wolves, bears and foxes, whom the few remaining people have started to hunt in their increasingly desperate search for food.

Then, just when it looks as though all manifestations of the All Life are withdrawing from the world altogether, they return. For the longest time, they seem almost to vie with the Great Cold, first one side seeming to gain precedence, then yielding it, then regaining it once more until finally the All Life in its many forms proves irresistible, pushing the snow and ice further and further back north and refilling the arid land as it does so.

But this time, almost as though in apology for its long

absence, the All Life appears as food-bearing grasses and trees of a kind not seen before: mainly wheat, but some barley and rye as well, and above all the hazel, its nuts appearing in great clusters every autumn. Animals soon follow, elk, roe and red deer, horse, pig, aurochs and finally, more people. Of course by then, almost all traces of the Lost Ones had been gone for a long time, or so we all used to assume.

The Great Cold is merely one of the many things that divide us from the Lost Ones—it's strange, but even now I don't feel entirely comfortable speaking to you about them—but another is how we see the relationship between the All Life and this world. Perhaps, before they suffered their terrible fate, the Lost Ones saw everything as a slow, relentless progression and therefore predictable. Perhaps they were even naïve and arrogant enough to believe that they had some measure of control over it. By contrast, we know it to be a far more complicated and wholly unpredictable process over which we have no control at all.

This is not merely because the Great Cold happened, but because by the time of which I'm about to tell you, it appears to be happening again. For the last hundred generations or so, manifestations of the All Life in our world on which we depend seem once again slowly to be withdrawing from it, allowing the Great Cold to creep back. First, pine and birch replace more oaks, ashes and elms. Then after a while, they too are replaced, this time by cold, dry grassland, so that the food to be found amongst the trees and bushes dwindles still further. The trees and the bushes have been our security and safety and, above all, the source of all our food for a very long time, as far back indeed as most lineages go. Yet now, it seems that the trees, even the hardy birches and our good friend the tough hazel, are slowly being driven out from the world by the creeping cold. And for a time, all we can do is stand and watch, terrified but helpless, like ants watching the man who may be about to tread on them without even knowing that they're there, as they scurry around in their panic beneath his gigantic feet.

But to go back to what I was saying just now, even if some

people believe that there might once have been a time when there wasn't a Traveller, no one knows of a time when our Traveller was not just there. And whether or not She has always been there, She is, as I said, unique. Everyone else will have their own particular talent, whether as a tracker, archer, butcher, tanner, wheat finder or whatever, although once a child's formal education is complete, he or she needs to be able to turn their hand to just about anything.

However, there are two specialist roles in the sense that those who undertake them can never do anything else: the Traders and the Law Sayers. This is because each one requires such lengthy training and, in particular, the most remarkable memory. Beyond trading goods, the Traders have to know every feature of every path between every village and every detail about everyone and everything in those villages. The Traders are also the principal means of communication between families who, as the women in them marry and go to live in their new husbands' villages, become widely dispersed. So the Traders must also be able to remember lengthy and detailed messages to take from one village to another. Indeed it is for this reason that some of the younger Traders are chosen to act as special messengers to and from the Traveller.

In a similar way, the Law Sayers have to know every Law in relation to everything, from food quotas to building materials and from goat rustling to trade agreements. They also have to interpret the Laws in the light of the messages brought back by the Traveller from the All Life. So first becoming, and then remaining, either a Trader or a Law Sayer is quite simply the work of a lifetime. Even so, there are still plenty of Traders, and each of the four Federations has at least five Law Sayers in it at any one time. But there has only ever been one Traveller.

This makes it still stranger that nearly everything else about the Traveller is a mystery. Until comparatively recently, the only people who have ever seen Her are the special messengers I referred to just now, the young women and men selected from the Traders to convey requests for the Traveller's advice and bring

Her advice back. And not even these messengers know where the Traveller originally came from, or even her actual name.

So needless to say, rumours about the Traveller abound. Most are a little wild and some are downright silly. But of the more believable rumours, one is particularly intriguing. This is that although the Traveller was born in an incredibly distant time, so distant in fact, and this is always relayed in a whisper, that She was taken to the House of Women when She was a young girl, She is actually very youthful-looking, and that this is because whenever She returns from only days in the All Life, years or even decades have passed in this world. Yet as I say, this is only a rumour. All that can be said about the Traveller with any certainty is that She lives alone in a house which is not part of any village but which stands by itself a long way to the north, half a day from the most northerly village of the Northern Federation.

However, before I tell you any more about the Traveller, or even about the child who used to be me and who somehow became a bird, I need to tell you more about our village and how we came to be where we were when all this happened.

*

I mentioned that our village is on one of the large hills near Verba and that it had moved there just before I was born. Verba has always done his best to help us, providing pike, tench, bream, salmon, roach, shad, perch and trout. There is duck, crane, cormorant, heron, swan and otter and beaver around his banks as well, but there is no question of relying on Verba alone for our food. As soon as a child can hold its head up, it is taken food gathering with its mother and so will begin the long task of learning about each type of fruit, berry, nut, seed, root, plant, insect, bird and animal.

A child's formal education begins as soon as it can crawl. The lessons start with the practical ones of what fruits, berries, nuts, seeds and roots are edible and which are not. Then they move on to which plants can be used for what kind of medicine and where each type is to be found, before covering things like what times in the year each type of plant is best eaten, if it's food, or applied fresh, if it's a medicine and what is best stored, how it should be stored and for how long. When the child has learnt all this, he or she will start learning how much of each type of food or medicinal plant must always be left so that it will continue to grow properly, and what to say to the tree or bush so that it knows we are grateful to it for allowing some of itself to be taken.

By the time the child is ten, she or he will be expected to have learnt not only all this, but also how to prepare the food and medicines, and finally, what Laws apply to each type of food or medicinal plant, the limits on gathering white acorns being just one example.

Any mistake after the probationary period between the Spring and Autumn Equinoxes following a child's tenth birthday will result in deep humiliation for both the child in question and his or her family. More seriously, it will also result in a delay in the commencement of that child's secondary education in fire keeping, flint knapping and our relationships with the insects, the birds, the fish and the other animals. Without that, the final part of a child's formal education, hunting if it's a boy and trapping if it's a girl, and in either case, how to prepare what has been hunted or trapped so as to ensure the continued goodwill of the animals in question, is quite impossible.

The subjects which children are taught are themselves dictated by the Law and so are common throughout all four Federations, although the way in which children are taught these subjects is a matter for the discretion of each individual village. The Federations themselves, and indeed the villages that comprise them, vary in size, the largest at this time being the Eastern Federation with nine villages, whereas I will be born in a village in the smallest, the Northern Federation, with only six. But again the Law dictates that each village in each Federation follows the same plan. All houses must be contained within an encircling ditch, outside which are the village's latrines, usually to the east as the prevailing winds are westerlies. Directly opposite them on the far side of the ditch to the west is each village's Station. Every village must be built either on a slight slope or on sandy ground, so that the houses and the outlying latrine facilities are properly drained, minimising the risk of contamination.

These and similar Laws ensure that all the villages are of a comfortable size and have a reasonable distance between them: far enough away from one another for there not to be too many squabbles, but close enough for immediate communication. Wolves can be troublesome now and again, pigs too for that matter, but apart from them, there aren't any really dangerous animals living with us amongst the trees. The lions and bears live much further to the northeast, close to the mountains, where it is said that on a clear day and if you are prepared to climb a tall pine, you can still see the Great Cold skulking on the summits. All in all, life would be good, except for the fact that each year there is less food than the year before.

This is how it has been for generations. Each year is slightly colder than the last, bringing new reports of more trees lost, and the cold, windy, open grassland known to everyone simply as the Sea of Grass getting that much closer, which is why each year there is less and less food. People are not starving, and the rate at which food supplies are dwindling is slow. Yet it is relentless.

For a long time, the feeling of sheer helplessness in the face of what seems to be the inevitable means that the subject is not even discussed, and some people decide that the best way of dealing with it is simply to persuade themselves that it doesn't exist. But finally, an extraordinary meeting of the Supreme Council, comprising senior members of the four Federation Councils and which usually meets every two years, is convened to debate one simple but terrifying question: what are we to do if we are not all to starve?

Some people, who are either very brave or very desperate, have already proposed to individual Federation Councillors that we should try to learn from the Lost Ones. After all, they say, before the Lost Ones vanished from the world, they clearly prospered, and could only have done so by building a successful relationship with the animals that surely lived with them in the strange treeless, stony deserts in which they are rumoured to have made their home. But this proposal is so firmly dismissed that it is unlikely ever to be made again. Since it is generally accepted that the Lost Ones brought infinite disaster upon themselves, any suggestion that we should attempt to emulate them in any way is regarded by most people as extraordinarily irresponsible. And in any case, since the All Life ousted the Great Cold and the world became warmer and the trees became our home, we have all grown so used to the food that until recently was so conveniently to be found amongst them that no one can really imagine trying to live any other way.

There is a further practical problem with trying to learn how to hunt or find other foods on the ever-expanding cold and windy Sea of Grass, which is that no one wants to go there. There are a few very old tales about the first onset of the Great Cold when wide open spaces containing nothing but grass first began to appear beneath the bright sun, endlessly glaring in the otherwise barren nothingness above. But these old tales give no sense of what such an open space actually looks like, and far more importantly, feels like. These things can be known only to the very few people who have been to the Sea of Grass, and they can never explain them to those who have not.

Yet that at least is set to change. The Supreme Council concludes that there is no option but to ask the Animals of the Sea of Grass, primarily the horses and the deer, if they will tell us how we may hunt in such a hostile environment. This means enlisting the help of the Traveller, because only She can go to the All Life, speak there with the true essence of the Animals of the Sea of Grass, and return. A messenger is duly sent to Her cold and lonely home, and shortly returns with the news that She has agreed to the request and in fact has already departed on Her journey to the All Life.

No one, not even the Traveller herself, knows when She will return to our world. There is therefore little to do whilst She is away but turn to the ancient stories to see if we can find any clue in them as to how we used to hunt on the open spaces during the Great Cold. As I say, there are only a few of these stories, and they have never before been understood as containing any actual instructions. Now we must consider them afresh to see what clues they may contain to help us re-learn the techniques that our distant ancestors used to track deer and horse under the open skies.

It is of course already apparent that these techniques will be very different to the ones we know. Our hunters are trained in how to move silently past the thickest undergrowth and how, when the prey breaks cover, to sprint through it without tripping to close in for the kill, using spears short enough for stabbing with all the upper body strength necessary to bring down a mature stag or stallion, yet long enough to keep clear of swinging antlers and lashing hooves. Now our hunters must find ways of tracking horse and deer over the Sea of Grass for days at a time so that old or young members of the herd become exhausted and agree, or even want, to be taken, and they must develop the stamina necessary to do so. New weapons must be designed and made, and our hunters must become proficient in their use. These include spear-throwers modelled on ancient ones obtained long ago from the nomads of the eastern desert, javelins with long slender points that will drive deep into the flesh of their target and more powerful bows that shoot lighter and differently fletched arrows for greater accuracy over longer ranges.

This takes a long time, but it is finally done. Yet all this effort will be wasted unless we can find a way to make clothing that can allow these newly acquired skills to be used in a shelterless place of endless wind and cold. For this vital piece of information, we have no choice but to await the return of the Traveller.

The only way in which the Supreme Council can know if the Traveller has finally come back from the All Life is by regularly sending messengers to Her house. Many are sent and return with no news but then finally, three years after Her departure, one messenger returns to say that the Traveller has come back, although it will later transpire that Her discussions in the All Life have taken no more than a few minutes. However, the Traveller's detailed report of those discussions, which this messenger also brings, and which is at once relayed via the Traders throughout all of the villages in all four Federations, makes for alarming, chastening and above all mystifying listening.

"We will help you to survive what is coming," the Traveller has been told by the Animals of the Sea of Grass. "We and our cousins who live with you amongst the trees have known for far longer than you people of the danger facing us all. You already know that the Great Cold is returning. What you do not know is that although it will not do so with the force of before, or to the same extent, yet it will still be more than enough to drive animals and people as you know them from the world."

The Traveller has been expecting bad news, but nothing as appalling as this. She is deeply shaken.

"Surely it cannot be so bad?" She asks eventually. "When the Great Cold came before, almost all the animals managed to survive, and we people did too. We did so by learning to make and control fire, to preserve meat, to build houses. To make proper clothing."

"But then you had not grown soft," the Animals of the Sea of Grass tell her. "You were not as pampered as you are now. You can no longer easily adapt to a changing world. It is clear to us, even if it is not clear to you, that you have forgotten how to change yourselves. You must remember how to do so, for only then can you learn how to change the world. You have no choice but to do this. Because only through doing this can you save us all."

"Then that is what we shall do," says the Traveller. "We will meet this threat as we met the last, animals and people together."

"We understand you rather better than you understand yourselves," is the bitter reply. "We will indeed give you all the help we can. But you will not be grateful. In fact, in return for our help, you will slaughter most of us, and those of us that you allow to remain, you will condemn to miserable captivity. Since we do not wish this, we do not wish to give you any help at all. We are only doing so because the alternative is to be thrust out of the world altogether."

Not only shaken but by now deeply ashamed, the Traveller

asks the Animals of the Sea of Grass if they can at least show us what it is that we are to look for.

"Do not expect us to provide you with answers to all your questions," She is told curtly. "If we do so, you will never begin to learn how to change yourselves and the world, as we have already said you must. All we will tell you is that your first venture onto the Sea of Grass will help show you the way that you all must go."

"But we cannot hunt on the Sea of Grass," the Traveller objects. "We are only now trying to learn how, but we do not know how to make the clothing that will allow us to move while still protecting us from the cold."

"But you have the means to learn. You simply do not know that you do. Our cousins whom you hunt and trap amongst the trees already provide you with what you need. It is all in their heads, and in ours. All you have to do is enter into them and be sure to make the very best use of what you find there."

There is yet another extraordinary meeting of the Supreme Council to consider the Traveller's report. Guided as usual by her advice, the conclusion is that there is no choice but to accept what the Animals of the Sea of Grass have said.

Yet there is a problem in that no one knows what this actually means. So the Supreme Council also decides that there must be an expedition to the Sea of Grass to see if any clues may be found there.

This takes a long time to organize, as it requires lengthy negotiations, not just between Federations but between villages in each of them. However, one is finally assembled, comprising twelve of the best hunters to have volunteered from all four Federations. When they are as ready as they can make themselves, they convene at the most northerly village of the Northern Federation, as that is the closest to the Sea of Grass. Shortly after that, they set off.

It has already been agreed that when the expedition reaches the end of the trees and the beginning of the Sea of Grass, it will divide into two groups. Eight of the hunters will form a base camp from which they will hunt amongst the remaining trees whilst the other four will leave those trees to venture onto the Sea of Grass itself. Only at this point will it be clear who will be in which group. Which members of the expedition, on being confronted with the terrifying openness for the first time, cannot go onto it, afraid that the bright unshaded sun will surely blind them, or even which of them will cling to the nearest tree, screaming that if they let go, they will fall upwards into the gaping emptiness above, will never be revealed to anyone else. This discretion is understandable, although probably unnecessary. No one would criticise anyone else for reacting like this, as no one else knows how they would feel if they were confronted with this strange and disturbing place.

Another precaution has already been taken, that of managing the expectations of those left behind. Well before the expedition embarks, each Federation Council has let it be known throughout their villages that the expedition will almost certainly not return with any actual kills from the Sea of Grass. There are several good reasons for why this will probably be so. First, we do not yet know the essence of the Animals of the Sea of Grass, particularly the horse and the deer, nearly well enough to hunt them. Second, we do not yet have any hides from the animals we will actually hunt, and it is only by putting them on as part of the hunt preparations that the hunters can acquire those animals' sense and feeling. Third, as the Traveller has explained to the Animals of the Sea of Grass, we do not have the right clothing. Even at Midsummer, no one can survive a night on the Sea of Grass without wearing several layers of otter fur, which is not only very expensive but far too heavy for the sudden, swift and silent movements essential for hunting.

Instead, each Federation Council makes it known throughout its villages that the purpose of the expedition is to gather information so that we can in time learn how we might hunt in what is for us a completely new environment. But the fact that this environment is so different makes it difficult to guess what the Animals of the Sea of Grass could have meant when they told the Traveller that something on this expedition would show us the way we have to go. Although everyone has carefully avoided calling this expedition a hunt, that is in a way what it is, the only difference being that this time, no one knows what is being hunted. Moreover, hunting involves closely scrutinizing your surroundings for things not usually seen, whether droppings of different consistency, an odd hoofprint pattern that could suggest lameness, even a broken branch where normally there would not be one. Looking for something strange in a place where everything is already strange is clearly impossible, so the hunters in this expedition quickly realise that they need to look for the unexpectedly familiar. And rather to their surprise, after a few days, the unexpectedly familiar is found.

Still with no sign of the herds of horses or deer rumoured to be grazing on the Sea of Grass, a hunter from one of the villages in the Western Federation is keeping his eyes fixed firmly on the ground as, hunched against the constant biting wind, he moves uncomfortably under the cold and terrifying bright nothingness.

Suddenly, he finds himself looking more closely at a large patch of grass. It is quite different to the unending featureless dun-coloured growth everywhere else and yet at the same time familiar. Then he recognizes it as wheat.

His village, like many others, tries whenever possible to gather the wheat that grows nearby so that in winter, when, as is now almost always the case, the previous summer's hunting has been poor and the salted meat has run out, there will at least be some bread. But the reason the hunter does not recognize the wheat straight away is that he has never seen it growing like this, in such profusion and over such a large area. Then he remembers that many years before, his great grandfather, speaking in a whisper for fear of being overheard, had told him something about the time of the Lost Ones. He said that most of the food the Lost Ones had in such abundance that they could keep everyone in their enormous villages made of huge stone houses fully fed, came from wheat. The hunter later confesses that at the time, he had dismissed this as nonsense. Everyone knows that wheat is one of the hardest foods to gather and that it is therefore extremely difficult to feed more than a few people with it. In any case, the hunter had been so embarrassed by his great grandfather talking about the Lost Ones that he had refused to listen to him a moment longer and had long since dismissed his tale. But right now, the sheer strangeness of the place in which the hunter finds himself, together with a keen awareness of just how much depends on this expedition, makes him wonder if there might not be something in the tale after all.

The hunter reports his find to the head of the expedition, and the precise location of the wheat is duly memorized. It is included in the expedition's formal report to the Supreme Council shortly after its return, along with the possible whereabouts of the horse and deer herds, their likely migration patterns and the best way to mount a proper hunt, of which animals and with what equipment. The Supreme Council then directs a second expedition to the Sea of Grass. Again, it is not a proper hunt, as we are still no nearer to solving the problem of the right clothing.

This time it will be a wheat gathering party.

At first, there is quite a lot of excitement about this discovery. Some villages have never gathered wheat at all, having none growing within their catchment areas, so they will have to learn from the villages that do how to make silos to store the modest amount of seed pods they have been able to gather. These silos are special pits with their walls covered with waterproofing: quicklime if this can be obtained from the Traders, and river clay if it cannot. The villages also have to learn how to turn the seed into bread. In so doing, they will also discover just how much effort it takes to grind the seed out of the seed pods and how much of it is needed to make a very modest amount of mush which can then be cooked on heated stones and made into flat, tasteless turd-like lumps of bread that when eaten still leave you feeling hungry, as well as picking stone grit from your teeth for days afterwards.

All in all, the initial excitement turns quickly to disappointment. But of course no food source can be ignored, however unappetizing or unsatisfying the food in question may be. So within a few years, summer wheat gathering expeditions become a part of life, albeit one heartily disliked by everyone. The bright, cold Sea of Grass continues to expand each year, but since it is still a long way away from the most northerly village of the Northern Federation, the wheat gathering parties are often away for almost as long as the hunters. And still, no one is ever really comfortable leaving the trees.

Another reason that wheat gathering is so unpopular is that the pickings are always so very meagre. The wheat growing on the Sea of Grass includes a strange variety not encountered before, where the seed pods do not fall from the stalks even when they are ripe. This variety can therefore be picked quite easily. Yet there is relatively little of it, and all too often the wheat gatherers arrive at the wheat patches after their long journey to the Sea of Grass only to find that the seed pods of the commoner type have already fallen from the stalks and been eaten by the birds, or are so ripe that they split open as soon as any attempt is made to pick them. Nor are we any closer to discovering how to make the clothing necessary for actual hunting on the Sea of Grass, because no one has guessed what the Animals were referring to when they told the Traveller that we need to make the best possible use of what they have in their heads.

Then, nearly three years after the Traveller's return from her meeting with the Animals bearing their cryptic message, a young woman from a village in the Northern Federation asks one of the Traders to pass a message of her own, direct to the Council of the Northern Federation. The young woman in question, Serris, has only recently arrived in this village following her marriage to one of its young men, Ulf. Most new wives in such a situation are very keen to fit into their new home without attracting any unnecessary attention, but it seems that Serris is not like most young wives, for she has asked the Trader in question, Gello, to tell the Council of the Northern Federation that she knows the meaning of the message from the Animals of the Sea of Grass, and that she must be taken to see the Traveller, so certain is she that she is right. Further, Serris absolutely refuses to say anything more to anyone else, to the point of facing down her furious young husband's repeated threats to beat more information out of her.

Naturally, everyone who hears of this assumes that this young woman is either delusional or simply mischievous and that the Council of the Northern Federation will ignore her impudent demands. Instead, the Council, within hours of receiving Serris' message from Gello, asks him to return to her with its agreement to her request, then to take a separate message to the remaining members of the Supreme Council convening yet another extraordinary meeting. This Supreme Council Meeting is then immediately adjourned to allow a small but well-armed group of hunters to escort Serris from her village to the Traveller's house in the far north, close to the edge of the Sea of Grass. There, the escort has to camp for two entire days, because that is how long Serris and the Traveller stay together in the Traveller's house, neither of them having any contact with anyone else the entire time.

Finally, Serris emerges from the Traveller's house alone. She tells her escort that the Traveller has confirmed her understanding of the meaning of the message from the Animals of the Sea of Grass. To their great irritation, however, she will not tell them what this is. It can, she says, be disclosed only to the Supreme Council direct. This, according to Serris, has also been endorsed by the Traveller.

By this time, nearly all the members of the Supreme Council have become very angry, feeling that they are being manipulated by this young woman. But however ridiculous they may feel, they also know that they will look far more ridiculous if, having gone along with all of this so far, they suddenly stop doing so. Also, they know just how much is at stake. Accordingly, they resume their adjourned meeting so that Serris can at last explain to them what the message of the Animals of the Sea of Grass actually means.

If her claim to have guessed the meaning of this message in the first place was surprising, the explanation of it that she finally gives is nothing short of astounding. It is that the way we have made clothes from animal skins for countless generations is, quite simply, wrong. Instead of tanning them with oak bark, dog dung and urine, we should use the animals' own brains. That is what the Animals of the Sea of Grass meant by going into their heads and making the best use of what we find there.

At this point, sorely tried tempers are close to being lost completely. Pressure for this upstart of a girl to be taught an unforgettable lesson grows to the point where one Supreme Councillor proposes obtaining an opinion from one of the Law Sayers on the harshest punishment possible. This is necessary, says the Councillor in question, to deter anyone from such presumption ever again. But the remaining Supreme Councillors have by now learnt just how stubborn this young woman can be. Far more importantly, they know that she now has the backing of the Traveller and that everyone else knows it too, particularly the Law Sayers themselves. So although everyone apart from Serris is far from happy, they know that they have no choice but to try the experiment.

Serris is therefore escorted back to her village where, with a Supreme Council observer, she awaits the next precious deer kill to be brought back to the village intact. In another unprecedented act, the hunters invite Serris to join them in formally obtaining the deer's consent to its own flaying and butchery. Once the deer has been flayed, butchered and the meat distributed, its hide is then tanned according to Serris' instructions, using the deer's own brains mixed with water taken from Verba, to whom the experiment has been explained and who has also agreed to it.

No doubt quite a few people have been eagerly anticipating the experiment's complete failure and the dire retribution that will swiftly be handed out to the young woman who has been so determined to try to make fools of so many. But such people are to be very disappointed, because when the hide dries out, it is softer and sweeter smelling than any anyone has ever seen, smelt or touched before. Better still, when water is poured onto it, it simply runs off. Best of all, it is completely windproof.

Within four months, enough horse and deer hides have been tanned in this way to make light, soft, supple, rain-resistant and windproof clothing to kit out an entire village hunting party, which at last can move across the Sea of Grass quietly and at speed. Within days, the hunting party returns with its first kill from the Sea of Grass, nothing less than a fine stallion. Within another few months, several more hunting parties have been similarly equipped, and by the end of the hunting season, the kill rate for the entire Northern Federation has risen to its highest level in almost thirty generations.

Through the Traders, the story of how our village was the first to make hunting gear from hides tanned using a solution of animal brain spreads throughout all four Federations. It is fair to say that the more people who hear the story, the more gaps and inconsistencies in it start to be commented upon. Some wonder how a young woman with no experience of tanning could have persuaded those who had been tanning for years that they had been getting it wrong all along. Others wonder how this young woman could have got the hunters to relinquish the animal brains, which have always been regarded as an important and immediate reward for a kill, to be given to the most deserving hunter at the discretion of the hunt leader. Others still wonder how anyone could have spotted something that for so many years had apparently eluded everyone else, including the Traveller Herself. Above all, people wonder what could have passed between the Traveller and this young woman in those two days that they spent together.

Of course in her own village, Serris is often asked these questions, but somehow, she seems able to avoid directly answering them. But then she is never pressed very hard to do so, first because this would somehow seem ungrateful, and second because there really isn't the time. We are already learning how to gather wheat in much greater quantities than before, and at last, with the right equipment and clothing, the hunters from all of the villages in the Northern Federation are beginning to hunt effectively on the Sea of Grass. Yet even though the number of kills from the Sea of Grass is rising, the rate of kills from our traditional hunting grounds amongst the trees is falling at a faster rate each year as the world grows colder and the Sea of Grass continues to push the trees back. So each year there is less and less good meat to go around. Rabbits and squirrels and such like are all very well, but you need an awful lot of them to feed a whole village, and the meat you get from animals such as otter and beaver really isn't very good for you, being so very lean. Without enough good fatty meat, fewer babies are born, and most of those that are born return to the All Life very soon afterwards. So, about two years before I arrive in the village, the Council of the Northern Federation decides that one of its villages must leave and join one of the other three Federations—if it can.

*

This decision is momentous because whichever village must move is going to find it very hard indeed. Before, everyone moved each year, usually around the Autumn Equinox and often more frequently still. However, it has been many generations since the advantages of staying in one place for years at a time outweighed the disadvantages, and to be honest we do rather look down our noses at the nomads of the eastern and southern deserts of whom the Traders have such entertaining tales. But this means that when we do have to move, it is much more of an ordeal.

Once the Council of the Northern Federation has taken this decision, there follow weeks of wrangling as to which village must leave. No Council member wants it to be their own, so the Council is unable to reach the necessary unanimous decision. This comes as no surprise, unlike its next step, which is to announce that it has sent a messenger to obtain the Traveller's advice. The surprise is due partly to the fact that this is tantamount to asking the Traveller to make the decision instead. According to the Law, all the Traveller can do is give advice, the Council to whom she has given it, whether a Federation Council or the Supreme Council, being obliged only to consider that advice, although in practice they have always accepted it. It is also surprising that the Council of the Northern Federation has bypassed the Supreme Council: previous requests for the Traveller's advice have always been made through the Supreme Council, so this looks like a deliberate snub. But what is most surprising of all is that the messenger sent by the Council of the Northern Federation to the Traveller is not one of the Traders, but Serris herself.

This last decision alone angers some Supreme Council members. Notwithstanding this, Serris, accompanied again by an armed escort, duly visits the Traveller to put this question to Her. It is widely assumed that in giving Her advice, the Traveller will take due account of factors such as which village is most likely to get permission to move to a new place from the Federation it wants to join, and how likely it is to survive the move. And there is little doubt that our village is best able to survive, because although all the villages in the Northern Federation have now learnt how to tan hides using animal brains, our village has the most experience and therefore still produces the best tanned leather by far, which means that we have something very valuable to introduce into the trading network of one of the other Federations. By the way, if you're wondering if I'm being a little inconsistent here, boasting when I say we make the best clothing, I can assure you I'm not, because everyone else says that we do. They will usually add that it's just as well that we can make such good clothing because we're hopeless at making anything else. That isn't actually true, but it's the sort of thing one is expected to put up with from time to time in order not to appear immodest.

Once again, Serris spends two days alone with the Traveller and returns with the Traveller's advice. This advice is that it is indeed Serris' own village—our village—that must move. The news is not exactly unexpected, but it still comes as a terrible blow. Also, it is impossible to ignore the sense of relief from everyone in all the other villages in our Federation, and equally impossible not to feel that relief as a form of rejection. Worse, it is only the start of what is going to be a very complex, protracted and painful process.

The first step in the process is formally to request permission from the Council of the Western Federation to join it. The Western Federation has the least acute food shortage, and its nearest villages are only three days to the southwest of our village's present location, which is why it has been identified as the most suitable. The Council of the Western Federation agrees to consider the request. Yet the preliminary signs are highly discouraging, as what our village can offer in terms of the Western Federation's market is seemingly outweighed by the fact that we will be more competition in its catchment area for less and less food. But then Serris lets it be known that the Traveller has advised not merely that our village should leave its existing Federation, but that it is the will of the All Life that our village should join the Western Federation.

This announcement is received with consternation, some unease and even some anger. The advice of the Traveller may always have been accepted, but it has always been sought first. Now it feels as though it is being imposed. More disturbing is the fact that no one has ever heard of the All Life expressing its will before, or indeed of the All Life having a will to express. Nor can anyone recall the Traveller ever referring to the All Life as a single entity.

It is of course the members of the Council of the Western Federation that feel most aggrieved, and they seek the advice of their Senior Law Sayer. But all he can do is remind them that the Law obliges them only to give due weight to the Traveller's advice, not to accept it, and despite a lot of grumbling, no member of the Council of the Western Federation is ultimately prepared to take the unprecedented step of suggesting that the Traveller's advice should be rejected. So at long last, proper negotiations over the terms on which our village can join the Western Federation begin.

Our village's negotiator will of course be Serris herself. Her renown as the one who deciphered the message from the Animals of the Sea of Grass when no one else, including the Traveller Herself, could do so has by now spread throughout the entire Trading network: from the fishing villages on the shores of the ocean in the west, to the nomads of the deserts in the south and east. Serris' influence within the village has therefore also continued to grow, not in the least affected by the recent death of her husband, Ulf. The big blood vessel in his thigh had been ripped open by the tusk of the pig he was trying to spear so that the child whom Serris is now carrying will be fatherless. But then Serris asks Bran if he will be her fellow negotiator. Bran is my father and the village's senior hunter. Later, when Arlen and I are a little older, we learn of his and Serris' role in what afterwards was always referred to just as the Move. We are far prouder of this than of the fact that Serris guessed the Animals' message or of my father's hunting prowess. We are wise enough to keep our pride to ourselves, unlike my sister Edra, who one day tells another little girl with whom she is arguing that our father is far more important than hers, for which our father thrashes her in front of all the other children to teach her better manners. Yet Arlen and I feel our pride in our respective parents to be justified, because although no one can remember when any village last had to move, everyone knows that the move will be very hard indeed, even assuming that the negotiations necessary for it to happen are successful.

Those negotiations will be difficult enough in their own right. They will also be very costly. Tanned hides and finished clothing that otherwise we would trade, tools and weapons and above all, food that is already scarce must all be presented to those whom we want to be our new neighbours. The finest such item is a special tunic made from the best brain-tanned deerskin, but it is not for any hunter. It is decorated with well over a hundred finely carved slivers of ivory from boar's tusks, which themselves took years of trading to accumulate. These slivers have been sewn onto the tunic so meticulously with such fine sinew, threaded through tiny holes drilled with delicate stone awls around the edges of each individual piece, that you have to study the tunic very closely to see any stitching at all. A few people are a little uncomfortable at the creation of so ostentatiously magnificent a garment, but then Serris explains that it will not be a gift to any individual Council member but to the Council of the Western Federation as a whole, and that it will be for them to decide who amongst them is the worthiest of it. In fact, it ultimately becomes the badge of office for the leader for the time being of the Council of the Western Federation, as Serris has no doubt anticipated.

Everyone, even the children, knows that items such as this should only ever be referred to as gifts, and never as goods or merchandise. But everyone also knows that is precisely what they are. They are goods that we have traded for the precious right to negotiate.

In addition to being expensive, the negotiations are protracted and slow. Rather to our surprise, we are informed by the Western Federation's Law Sayers that if the exact location of the village can be agreed, the Law will allow us first refusal of all growing food within a thousand paces of it. But just about everything else has to be settled through negotiation. We must agree which birches we can use to build our houses and of course our Station, where our Station will be located, which of the animals that live amongst the trees we can hunt, when we can hunt them, where, when, and for what animals we can set traps on the land, what other food we can gather, and again, when and where. We have to agree where on Verba in the two months either side of Midsummer we can have our fish traps, when, and how large they can be.

Above all, we must agree how, in the extremely unlikely event of there being any food above the agreed quota in any month, it is to be shared.

There follow months of persuading, demanding, cajoling and conceding and, as I mentioned a moment ago, bribing. And all this must be done over a three-day distance, with not merely Serris and Bran, but other Elders and the necessary armed escorts travelling back and forth to gather information, make trades, report back and take instructions, all in deteriorating weather, as Midwinter is getting dangerously close. Nor is there any certainty that any of these negotiations will be successful.

Many begin openly to question whether the Move will happen at all. But then, only a few days before the Winter Solstice, Serris returns from yet another session with the Council of the Western Federation to announce that satisfactory terms have at last been agreed. These terms include several arranged marriages. This last part is a largely symbolic gesture of commitment to our new neighbours, given that the children in question will in all probability either not be born at all or, if they are, will not be here long enough actually to marry. However, as symbolic gestures go, it is a very important one.

Two days after the conclusion of the Winter Solstice celebrations, the Court of the Western Federation is formally convened, and the agreed terms are proclaimed by the Senior Law Sayer of the Western Federation in the sight and hearing of representatives of the Elders from all of the villages in it. The proclamation takes almost all of the few daylight hours available, but everyone accepts that there is no alternative: the Law cannot work unless everyone agrees that ignorance of it is no justification for breaking it, so there can be no good reason for such ignorance in the first place. An allegation of a breach of the agreed terms will therefore immediately be referred back to the Law Sayers. If the Law Sayers uphold the allegation, they will give their opinion as to exactly how the terms have been breached and therefore what remedial action the Law requires. This usually means that the offenders' village will be fined, tradeable goods and even food being taken and used to compensate the village that has been wronged. The manner in which this may be done, and in particular which guilty individuals should be punished and how, are matters for the Elders of the village that has been fined. However, the Law Sayers may be asked by the Elders of that village for their advice on appropriate penalties, and these can range from a beating to a non-crippling mutilation or even, in the most serious cases, death.

So, at long last, the complex process of actually moving thirty-two households can get underway. We must first wait until after the Spring Equinox, as the move will be difficult enough in fair weather, but at least this allows time to recruit and organize two labour gangs. These will largely be comprised of volunteers from families in villages in the Northern Federation, the one we are about to leave. This is because our village simply does not have enough able-bodied adults to carry out the necessary work, herd our sheep and goats to our new home, and help the young and old make the journey.

The task of the first labour gang is to dismantle our Station and rebuild it in its new location. This is easily the most delicate part of the actual business of moving, although the need for the move has been explained to the Station's current residents by their families, and their agreement to it obtained: the residents themselves will of course make the move with their families.

The task of the second labour gang is to go on ahead to the village's new location in the Western Federation. There, they will start preparing the timber, wicker fending, twine, heather rope, and reed thatching that will be needed immediately upon the arrival of the rest of the village, so that pens for the sheep and goats can be constructed, and the rest of the necessary building work can start promptly. This second gang will be accompanied by some of the village Elders, whose task it is to agree terms with the birches whereby some of them will be felled, both to clear the new site and to use the timbers in the construction of the new houses. Only a few timbers can be reused from the houses we are leaving, as most are simply too large and heavy to be carried to the new site. These, together with our discarded reed thatching, will be left as a parting gift to whoever amongst our former neighbours may have a use for them, as we obviously can't take them with us, we would look dreadfully mean if we tried to trade them.

Next, the movement of our sheep and goats has to be organized. This needs to be done in two stages, as some of the goats' milk will be needed in our village's existing location until everyone has left it, and since the sheep and goats have to be herded, fed, and milked during the journey, it will take significantly longer than three days.

Once this is underway, the families themselves can begin to move. Each family group must include two able-bodied and well-armed adults, so some have to be joined by additional volunteers, again usually family members from other villages in the Northern Federation. The movement of these family groups has to be carefully coordinated with the movement of our sheep and goats and of course with one another. Since each group must also carry all their possessions themselves and will include young and old members, they too will take significantly longer than three days to complete the journey to our new home. Some will not complete it at all.

Those who do arrive find our Station re-erected in its new location, with over half of our sheep and goats in new pens and well-chosen plots for the new houses. Each plot has been carefully marked out with pegs and rawhide strips, and a few houses are actually in an advanced state of construction.

Prior to this, it has been generally assumed that lots will be drawn to see who will get the coveted central locations. However, in a spontaneous gesture of gratitude, the new Senior Village Elder, Morten—old Poric having returned to the All Life during the Move, as so many have—proposes that these should be awarded to Serris and Bran. Most people agree and those who do not are too tired to say so. The remaining sites are indeed allocated by lot, and despite a little squabbling, the construction of the houses continues at a respectable pace.

Building a house is a complex and time-consuming business, but although it has been a long time since we have had to build so many houses all at once, it is not the kind of thing easily forgotten. Soon the younger children are trampling the mud and dung to make the daub to go between the hazel-wand wattle that has to be weaved around the outer posts. This can be done by some of the older children, but only under the strict supervision of an adult: every tapered hazel wand has to be tensed first to ensure that there are no cracks, and then each has to be alternately placed end-on-end so that the finished wall will not develop fractures due to the irregular stresses within it.

Only adults who are particularly skilled at finding the right kind of wood within a growing birch can then be trusted to cut and shape them into the necessary rafters and purlins. These rafters and purlins will support the new reed thatching, which turns out to be of far better quality than the thatching we have been obliged to leave behind, having dried out remarkably quickly and being so tough that it probably will not need replacing for over twenty years.

Whilst there is naturally huge relief at having completed the actual journey, the construction period presents fresh dangers of its own. Little Dana is hit by an inadequately secured door post which topples onto her, breaking her wrist, and young Madoc falls through an incomplete roof, banging his head on the ground and getting quite badly concussed. However, after only a couple of weeks, all of the houses are complete, and families can leave the crowded and by now stinking tents and move into them, beginning with those relatives who must be carefully positioned in exactly the right place within the new home, usually by the front door. And at last, the village has a new home worth the name.

All in all, the completion of the Move is without a doubt a truly remarkable achievement and the esteem in which Serris and my father are held in our village increases accordingly, although both are shrewd enough to be appropriately self-deprecating. However, their standing soon increases still further. Less than a month after the last house is completed, a man and a woman arrive with an armed escort, a rather fierce-looking archer. Each of them is wearing a very finely embroidered deerskin cloak showing that they are a delegation from the Council of the Western Federation. First, they pay their respects to the residents of our new Station and then are taken on a short tour of the rest of the new houses. They politely admire these, but as they are here on official Council business, they are soon closeted with the village Elders. Later that day, after they have left, all of the village, even the children, are summoned to the central fire to hear the news. This is that the Council of the Western Federation has invited Serris to join it and asked my father to become the Federation Hunt Master, and that both have accepted these respective positions.

These are truly great honours, not just for Serris and my father but for the village as a whole, and everyone is very gratified. However, quite a few people are also a little puzzled as to how Serris and my father could have come to be held in such high regard by the Council of the Western Federation so very quickly. It soon becomes generally accepted that this is partly the result of the Traveller's report that it is the will of the All Life that our village should join the Western Federation, but mainly because in the course of the negotiations, the Council of the Western Federation immediately recognised that both Serris and my father possess exceptional qualities. This part of the explanation of course comes from Serris herself, but she manages to communicate it in such a subtle way—a knowing look here and a comment or two there— that very few people guess this. Later I learn that it is indeed true when finally I find out what Serris and my father have actually done to make themselves so indispensable.

Although we have reached agreement with our new human neighbours and with the birches in the immediate vicinity, we still have to come to an understanding with the land, water, the rest of the trees, and the animals in our new home. We have no guarantee that they are going to be friendly, so we must take every precaution to try and ensure that they are. Before the first fire is lit, we thank them for allowing us to live amongst them. We take special care to thank all the other nearby trees. Not doing so would be to risk insulting them, although the risk probably is not great, as the trees are far more likely to be preoccupied by the prospect of being driven out of the world by the falling temperature and the ever-spreading Sea of Grass.

As I just mentioned, there is a huge sense of relief on completing the Move. Still, no one believes that life in our new home is about to become easier, as we have moved not in the hope that things may improve, but in the hope that they may not get very much worse. Hunters must still venture onto the Sea of Grass for any decent sized kills and are therefore away for longer and longer. They still hunt the pigs, deer and elk that live with us amongst the trees and even the occasional aurochs. But all of these are increasingly rare and, as the death of Serris' husband Ulf shows only too well, pigs in particular have always been very difficult and dangerous to hunt, even with the right skills, which some of our hunters—the ones who do not venture onto the Sea of Grass— are only now trying to acquire. There is therefore no choice but to continue supplementing the food supply with whatever other meat might be available. We even eat the otter and beaver that used to be trapped only for their pelts to make clothes to trade for stone and antler, although their meat is so very lean that it must be carefully rationed so that no one becomes ill.

We also continue to gather wheat. Some wheat continues to grow amongst the trees, but far more grows on the Sea of Grass, so every summer, wheat gathering parties glumly set off to return days or sometimes even weeks later with their modest pickings. In addition, there is still the food that has always grown amongst the trees, but as there are fewer trees with the Sea of Grass continuing to advance, this continues to dwindle. We have a little more fish and duck than we had before, and even the occasional swan, but all of this is still nowhere near enough to replace the horse and the deer that had once been so plentiful.

Only six babies are born living in the first winter in our village's new home, including Serris' daughter, Arlen, and myself. By the following winter, there is so little good meat that someone suggests eating some of our goats and sheep and even the village dogs. This is of course a ridiculous idea. The goats and sheep produce more food alive than dead, and it is the dogs that keep rats down and the wolves from coming right up to the houses in their search for food. We also need their dung for tanning, brain being still too scarce to use it for anything other than hunting gear. Moreover, we have named all our goats, sheep and dogs as a mark of the agreement we have with them, so that killing them for food would be the most heinous violation of that agreement. The suggestion itself is therefore not taken seriously, but the fact that it has been made at all shows how alarmed people are becoming.

And all this is many years before we learn of the first of the Massacres.

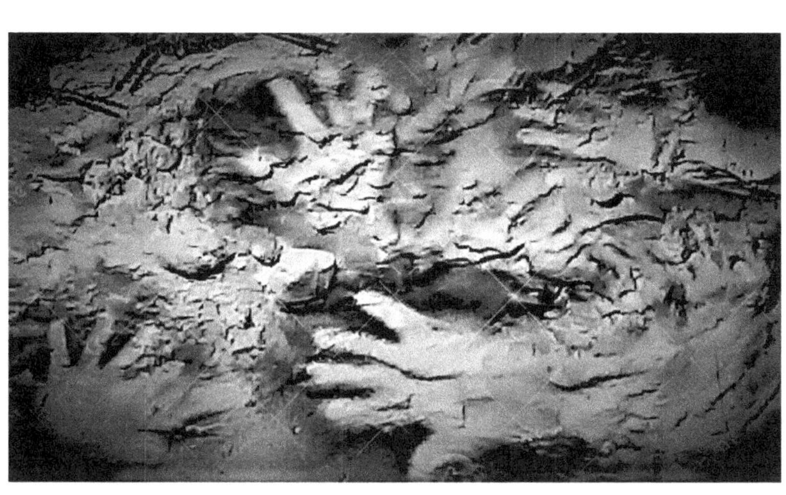

Six years after Arlen and I have been born, and the Spring Equinox has marked the beginning of the hunting season and the paths through the trees become largely passable again, the first of the year's Traders arrive. They bring weapon- and tool-quality stone, salt to help preserve what little meat we have left, quicklime for plastering our grain silos and, in the unlikely event that any is left over, the walls of some of our houses. The Traders may even bring a few more exotic items such as amber and carved quartz that can be stitched onto our best deerskins to create garments that more and more people want to wear on their last journey to their village Stations. Perhaps most importantly of all, the Traders bring news and messages, particularly for the women who became part of our village when they got married, from the families and friends they left behind.

These particular Traders are led by Gello. Since playing his part in the famous story of how Serris guessed the message of the Animals of the Sea of Grass all those years before, Gello has gone on to become the most experienced Trader throughout all of the Federations. Having visited villages from those in the Southern Federation nearest to the desert to those in the Northern Federation closest to the Sea of Grass, he has goods of unequalled variety to trade, although sometimes not quite of the quality he tries to make out. And since he is also rumoured to be nearly fifty years old, to all us children Gello has the further appeal of being fascinatingly ancient.

Every visit by the Traders follows a fixed routine. As soon as they arrive, each of them is surrounded by children all clamouring for presents, their parents making only the most half-hearted attempts to stop them. Most children gather around Gello. As they do so, he draws himself up to his full height—he may be very old, but he is still a tall and impressive-looking man—and glares down at them all in apparent outrage from beneath his magnificently shaggy eyebrows. Then, still scowling furiously, he turns and delves into his rucksack and pulls out handfuls of toys. These he distributes to the children, as do his four fellow Traders who, unlike Gello, cannot keep up the act and are all grinning broadly.

These toys are tiny figures, usually animals, deer, lions and horses, but sometimes some curious hybrids as well, all made by the more elderly members of the villages the Traders have already visited. They are in the main quite crudely crafted things of twigs and twine, but all are received by the squealing children with utter delight and will be played with incessantly until they fall to pieces a few days later.

This short but joyous little ritual is a prelude to a far more serious matter: the relaying of news and other messages from the villages through which the Traders have passed. This is without a doubt the most important skill that the Traders possess, and one that requires the training that effectively takes a lifetime. No matter how detailed and complicated the messages each Trader is asked to convey, he or she will recall them perfectly and will relay them word for word.

The first who are entitled to receive their messages are the residents of our Station. The Traders are duly led there by Morten, as our village's new Senior Elder. What the Traders have to tell the Station's residents is of course confidential, so Morten leaves them until Gello sends word to him via one of his junior colleagues that they have finished. The Traders then return to the village proper and visit every household for whom they have news and messages from their families, which takes several hours. Even though what the Traders may have to relate is again confidential to the recipients, it is very often that relatives and friends have returned to the All Life. This is why the next formal part of the Traders' visit is the adding of their Fire by their Fire-Keeper to the central fire of the village. The Traders' Fire is the accumulation of the light received from the central fires of all the villages in all the Federations which the Traders have previously visited. Once it has been added to ours, those who look to see the relatives and friends they will not see anywhere else in our world can, if all else fails, still find them there.

That leaves the general news and the information that everyone is entitled to hear. This will be announced before the village's central fire by Gello himself, as the Senior Trader. And although he has been in the village for only a relatively short time, Gello has already dropped a few hints that he has something particularly dramatic to relate. He turns to face his expectant audience and begins to speak.

At first, what he has to say is disappointingly predictable. The rate at which the Sea of Grass is encroaching from the north continues to accelerate. The levels of the kills of the hunting parties of all the Federations from amongst the trees continues to fall at a much faster rate than the rate of kills from the Sea of Grass is rising, so that, as with the year before, and every year before that, there is overall another small but perceptible decline. The birth rates of all the villages in all four Federations are therefore also continuing to fall.

Finally, Gello comes to the item that he has clearly decided to keep until last. He begins quite casually, telling how only a few weeks earlier he was commissioned with brokering a marriage at a gathering in the Southern Federation. He tells how he duly found a man who would have been prepared to marry the girl in question but for Gello's stipulated bride-price of two obsidian dagger-blades. The man finds this price far too high: not for the first time, Gello has rather over-estimated the strength of his bargaining position. It is clear from the faintly aggrieved tone in which Gello relates this part of his story that he does not accept this, which causes some rather ill-mannered tittering from his audience. But the tittering abruptly stops when Gello suddenly shuts his eyes, signalling that he has gone from the mere telling of a casual anecdote to a detailed word for word recitation of which only the Traders are capable.

What Gello begins to recite is the strange and horrible story that the man of whom he has just been speaking told him in between their many bouts of haggling. A few weeks earlier, so this man says, some people appeared in his village, people from the southernmost village of the Southern Federation. Most of these people have terrible wounds, and all of them are utterly exhausted. They claim to be the survivors of what, from their description, sounds like a hunting ambush but with their village itself as the quarry. These people say that their village has been destroyed by a group of men who just appeared one night, shot the village lookouts and then shot or cut the throats or smashed in the heads of everyone in the village they could catch, before setting fire to all the houses.

Gello abruptly stops speaking and opens his eyes so that he can enjoy his audience's reaction, which is the most sincere and gratifying kind possible: a collective gasp followed by stunned silence. He lets the silence continue for several long moments and then adds, perhaps a little pompously, that he himself finds this story very hard to believe. Nearly everyone quickly and enthusiastically concurs, relieved to be able to dismiss so very disagreeable an idea. But then someone somewhere in his audience says something to the effect that when food is short, people are bound to start killing each other.

Strangely, everyone gathered around the central fire that evening listening to Gello's bizarre and horrifying story will later remember this comment, but no one will recall who actually said it. Then again, perhaps that is to be expected, since it is received with even greater shock and disbelief than Gello's story itself. There are many Laws relating to food, what you can get, how you can get it and above all, how and when you are to share it. Some Laws are particular to certain Federations because they have been agreed by the Council of the Federation in question. Other Laws apply everywhere because they always have, although no one seems to know precisely how or why: formidable as the knowledge of the Law Sayers is, it is still sometimes hard to tell what the Laws actually are or how they work and why, in a few cases, they exist in the first place. Yet everyone knows that the Laws are there. So the suggestion that some people have decided to not just ignore them, but actually to kill other people so that they don't have to share their food is nothing short of outrageous. But what really upsets all the people there that night is the strong suspicion that this shocking, scandalous and deeply offensive suggestion is almost certainly correct.

Later that same evening, my mother Frey welcomes Gello to our house, where he will be our guest for the duration of the Traders' stay in our village. Gello has always been very welcome in our village, but not quite everyone looks forward to his visits. Although relations between Gello and Serris are perfectly courteous, most people have noticed that each of them always manages to arrange things so as to avoid the other as much as possible. It is widely believed that this has something to do with what passed between the two of them so many years earlier regarding the message from the Animals of the Sea of Grass. However, as neither Serris nor Gello will acknowledge this awkwardness, much less discuss the reasons for it, this remains mere speculation.

My father Bran is away with the hunting party, but there are several reasons why it is nonetheless perfectly seemly for Gello to stay at our house. First, my father, as Federation Hunt Master, is now one of Gello's most important customers for weapon-quality stone, including, when Gello can get hold of it, obsidian, which can be honed to an edge far sharper than any flint. Second, my mother knows quite enough about weapon-quality stone to make a very good bargain in my father's absence. Third, Gello is so old and so well known by everyone that there is no question of my mother requiring any kind of chaperone.

Arlen is staying at my house too, but then she is far more often there than she is in her own home, with her mother Serris being always so busy and, as I say, keen to be anywhere except wherever Gello happens to be: tonight, for example, she is beginning negotiations with the remaining Traders, along with the other village Elders.

When Gello arrives in our house, my mother formally welcomes him, and he formally thanks her for her and Bran's hospitality. Arlen stands next to my mother, head politely bowed, waiting for Gello to remove his cloak and hand it to her. As usual, I hang back in the shadows. Arlen and I are very excited at the prospect of getting a really good look at Gello's cloak. Unlike everyone else, whose life summaries are merely sewn onto their tunics, Traders have theirs stitched onto their long cloaks which can therefore be far more detailed. Gello's cloak is said to be the most detailed and consequently the most impressive of all, and we are not disappointed. We both gasp as we look at the intricate loops and spirals of the most delicate stitching of fine gut, each line showing one of Gello's many adventures. But even more exciting than Gello's wonderful cloak are the six strips of delicately carved antler that the removal of the cloak has revealed, each one hanging from Gello's belt by rawhide thongs threaded through a finely bored hole. These antler strips are maps of the principal trade routes along which Gello has travelled. Since each Trader knows every one of these long routes intimately without reference to any map, these are not so much practical aids as powerful symbols of a Trader's knowledge and indeed of his or her reputation. Like everyone else, Arlen and I have often heard of these exotic objects, but we have never seen one before. I gaze at them, longing to touch them, but then Gello clears his throat rather pointedly, and with a muttered apology and a red face, Arlen turns and walks quickly to the shadowy wall of the house where space for Gello's cloak has already been made on one of the shelves. There, she places the cloak reverently and she and I sit ourselves down well away from the two adults, watching them both intently.

First, Gello eats the food that my mother has offered him. There is embarrassingly little of it, but of course Gello is far too courteous to make any adverse comment. Then, as Arlen and I continue to watch fascinated from the shadows, Gello and my mother sit down opposite one another across the fire and the serious business of the evening begins.

Gello reaches down to his battered goatskin knapsack and rummages in it for a few moments. Then he brings out a dark lump of stone which he hands to my mother with an air of confident expectation. She takes it from him and, holding it near to the fire, examines it closely for a few moments. Then she hefts it a few times, purses her lips and nods.

"It's a good weight," she concedes. She holds it closer to the fire, peering at it once more. "But I'm going to need to see it in daylight."

"Of course, madam," replies Gello, politely inclining his head towards her. "And I welcome the opportunity for you to do so. But you surely need no daylight to feel the evenness of the planes. Smoother than the cheek of a newborn child. As you will know well, that tells you that there are no fractures, no internal stresses, no imperfections of any kind in the stone. This stone will yield three, four, perhaps even five hunting blades of the very finest quality. In the right hands, of course."

My mother has dealt with Traders often enough to know never to be drawn into making any comment about their goods so early in the negotiations. I can also see that she is bristling slightly at Gello's reference to the lump of flint yielding up to five blades in the right hands. A year earlier, Gello traded a similar piece of high weapon-quality stone to my father, who, in trying to make the first spear blade from it, promptly smashed the stone so completely that all that could be salvaged were a few arrowheads. No one has ever directly criticised my father for his mediocre flint knapping abilities, because he is the finest hunter in the Federation and nobody is good at everything. It's the fact my father won't admit that he is not a very good flint-knapper that my mother finds rather exasperating. That said, she resents anyone else pointing this out or even alluding to it, as Gello just has. But then again, she knows how Gello often uses his talent for delicate offensiveness to put the person with whom he is negotiating at a disadvantage. So the only answer she gives him is a polite if rather cold smile and the awkward pause that ensues gives Arlen the chance that she and I have been waiting for.

"I'm sorry to interrupt," Arlen says to Gello very politely. "But can I ask why you said what you did earlier, when you told us about all those people who were murdered? Why did you say that you didn't believe it?"

My mother's mouth opens in surprise as she turns quickly to stare at Arlen. At first, it seems to me that she is angry at Arlen's presumption in speaking to Gello without being invited to do so. Then I see that the expression on her face is not one of anger, but one of dismay mingled with fear. However, in another moment it has turned to anger, and suddenly my mother is on her feet. She takes two swift strides towards Arlen, hand raised as though about to strike her. Arlen steps back, reaching for me. Then my mother stops. Gello has cleared his throat again, loudly and even more pointedly than before. My mother looks back at him in surprise.

"Do please forgive my presumption, madam" says Gello, courteously but firmly. "Far be it from me to interfere. But if I may say so, I do not believe the child intended any disrespect."

It seems to me that my mother is unwilling or unable to hold Gello's steady and politely challenging gaze. Then she looks back at the frightened but unabashed Arlen and, although she scowls at her again, lowers her hand and steps back to Gello and the fire. Gello smiles at them both in an attempt to ease the tension and then beckons to Arlen. She steps over to the fire, and of course I follow her. The light inside the house is so dim and Gello's white brows are so bushy that I can't make out his eyes, but both Arlen and I know that they are far sharper than those of many people a third of his age. He looks at Arlen for quite a long time, studying her. The polite smile has now gone, leaving his wrinkled face quite expressionless. We look back at him, excited but also very apprehensive. He opens his mouth to speak but then shuts it again when my mother suddenly drops several otter pelts next to the lump of flint that the two of them have just been discussing. Gello looks at the pelts for several moments. Then he looks at my mother, frowning as though deeply puzzled. Suddenly his frown clears, and he smiles broadly again. He nods slowly.

"Ah yes, madam. I see. Your implication that these sorry, moth-eaten remains are somehow of comparable value to the best weapon-quality stone is clearly a jest. How very foolish of me not to see it straight away. Most amusing. Although if I may say so, it is perhaps a little unkind of you to make a simple old Trader the butt of your exquisite and subtle wit."

His smile vanishes as he turns contemptuously away from my mother's admittedly poor-quality otter pelts and back to Arlen.

"Let me see," he says. "Ah yes. You are Arlen, daughter of

Serris and Ulf. You were six on the seventeenth day of the third month. Your father returned to the All Life before you were born, courtesy of a hunting wound inflicted by a particularly foul-tempered boar."

Arlen smiles and nods. Like me, she knows perfectly well that none of what Gello has just said is remotely relevant, but that like all Traders, he does like to show off his remarkable memory.

"I believe that what I actually said earlier," Gello continues, "was that I found the story told to me by the man of whom I spoke difficult to believe. Is that what you are asking me? Why I find it difficult to believe?"

Arlen and I nod in unison. Gello sighs.

"Well, first of all, because the thing that he described is so utterly unheard of. And if I may say so without sounding immodest, if I haven't heard of such a thing before, I doubt if anyone else has."

He sits back and spreads his hands.

"Of course, now and again one hears of a village lookout being knocked on the head when a few goats go missing. Or of skirmishes between hot-blooded, foolish young men in different hunting parties before older and wiser men can step in. Such things are inevitable, although no less regrettable and unpleasant for that. But we have learnt how to deal with them. Everything is reported to the Law Sayers, who tell us precisely in what way the Law has been broken, what needs to happen for things to be put right, and the Federation Councils and the Elders of the villages in question see that it is done. In most cases, an appropriate fine, followed by a reconciliation meeting and a few peace-oaths, will resolve matters. In some of the more serious cases, there may even have to be a flogging or a couple of facial mutilations. I can even remember an execution, let me see, yes, ten years and four months and seventeen days ago. There was a man, Ettan, son of Marli and Dorn, twenty-two years old, from the fourth village of the Eastern Federation. He stole food from the grain store in the neighbouring village."

All three of us gasp simultaneously in horror.

"Oh yes," says Gello, after a suitable pause. "He was duly convicted, and the first part of his sentence was that he should be tied to a wicker fence and put face down into a bog between his village and the neighbouring one from which he had stolen the food. Three of his fellow villagers stood on the other side of the fence until he drowned. Obviously, he did so quite quickly. The rest of his sentence was that he should be left in the bog. Which I suppose is where he is to this day."

Gello smiles grimly at the reminiscence. Then his frown returns.

"But the planned destruction of a village and the murder of everyone in it?" Slowly, he shakes his shaggy white head. "That is altogether different. Never in all my long years of trading have I heard of anything so—"

He stops, uncharacteristically lost for the right word.

"So wicked," he goes on at last. "And quite apart from the sheer wickedness, what would be the point? What could anyone possibly hope to gain by doing such a thing? It's not as though you could do anything with what was left after a village was destroyed. You wouldn't know the land, or the water, or any of the animals. And you can take my word for it that no one in any of the other villages in any other Federation would ever trade with you. You'd starve in weeks."

Gello sits back.

"So that is why I say I find it very hard to believe."

There is silence for a few moments. Then Arlen speaks.

"I know it is very hard to believe," she says quietly. "And yet it is true."

The house is already still, as is the rest of the village outside, but suddenly there seems to be a different kind of stillness in it. Gello stares at Arlen again. Then he reaches out and beckons to her with his hand once more.

"Come here, child," he says softly.

Looking calm and not at all frightened, Arlen steps towards him. Gello's wrinkled old hand descends gently onto her shoulder and he looks steadily into her eyes for a long time.

"You know this?" he asks finally. "You promise me that you know this?"

Arlen nods, holding Gello's gaze.

"Yes. We know this. We know this because we have seen it."

"And we have heard it," I add, despite the fact that neither Gello nor my mother is paying me the slightest attention.

Although he is doing his best to disguise it, Arlen and I can see that Gello is profoundly affected in some way by what Arlen has just told him. He swallows, and again his usual garrulousness seems to desert him. For a long time, he is silent, and then finally, he nods slowly.

"Very well."

My mother, who has been staring at Arlen, suddenly turns to him, astonished.

"You don't mean to tell me that you believe her?" she demands, her voice quavering and ever so slightly too loud.

Gello raises his eyes from Arlen and looks at my mother. Then he frowns, and when at last he speaks it is clear that he is choosing his words with great care.

"As you are well aware, madam, the polite term for much of what we Traders do is negotiating. The more accurate, if somewhat blunt description, would be lying and being lied to. Whatever one chooses to call it, it means that I have learnt to recognise the truth when I hear it. What this child has just told me is very obviously true. So of course I believe her."

My mother stares at him but does not answer. Gello's eyes remain fixed on her, but then something in his expression changes. "I wonder how you can be so certain that you do not," he adds quietly.

*

By the time Arlen and I are eight, every single village in the Southern Federation has been destroyed and almost every person in them murdered, each time the men responsible vanishing as mysteriously and as suddenly as they first appear.

The adults in our village do their best to try and reassure all the children that this will not happen to us or to any village in the Western Federation. However, these attempts have very little effect. This is mainly because most of the adults are so obviously frightened themselves, not just by the horror of what has happened but by their sheer powerlessness in the face of it. Many keep repeating that surely the Law Sayers will do something about it, despite it being clear to everyone that there is nothing that the Law Sayers can do. Even though the children are disturbed by their parents' fear, most are more thrilled by the drama rather than scared of something they cannot really understand. All of the children, that is, except for Arlen and me.

As Arlen has told Gello, we have already seen the very first of what will become known as the Massacres. What she did not tell Gello, and what we have not told anyone else, even my brothers Breccan and Rod, is that each of us has seen and heard every single death. We have seen each arrow find its target and heard the strange and horrible sound when they do so, slicing through flesh and thudding into bone. We have seen each axe smash into the heads of every woman and child and heard the screams changing from those of mere frightened surprise to those of helpless terror as the victims suddenly realise what is happening to them.

Yet our experiences of the next Massacre and the ones following that are far worse in that we do not just see and hear what is happening to the victims: somehow, we feel it as well. We share in their shock and terror, their agonizing pain and their helpless misery. And what turns out to be the last of these experiences is the most dreadful of all.

Although we are asleep in our village, we are somehow also living in a different village somewhere in the Southern Federation. In this village it is night too, but this time we are wide awake, holding onto one another and sobbing in fear. We can hear men shouting and women and children screaming. We see torches coming close and we know that the men holding them have come to kill us all. An elderly man we seem to know very well—it may be my grandfather, but as I'm not really me, I can't be sure—takes each of us by the shoulder. He pushes us hard in the opposite direction, shouting at us to run, to run as fast as we can. But then he makes a funny gasping noise and falls to the ground, two arrows protruding from his back. For a moment, my friend and I stare at the dead body in shock, but then fear takes over again, and still holding one another's hands tightly, we begin to run. A man carrying an axe in one hand and a spear in the other sees us and begins to chase after us. We are far too little to stand any chance of outrunning him, and I hear him grunt with effort as with a wild swipe of his axe he hits me on the back of my head. The pain is unbelievable, far, far worse than any pain I have ever felt before, yet somehow, I manage to stumble on for a few more steps before I too fall. I have to get up and start running again to get away from this man who I know is determined to kill me. But I can feel myself getting weaker as the blood pours from the wound in my head, and I can't make my arms and legs move. Suddenly I know with complete certainty that I am about to die. I am very afraid of dying, but I am also angry because it is so unfair that I should die like this, killed by someone I have never even met, let alone harmed in any way. But all of that lasts only an instant because then I feel a different kind of fear flooding over me, the fear that my friend is feeling: she is terrified for herself, but far more afraid for me, and has stopped running. I try to shout at her not to stop, to keep on running, to get away, but by now I am so weak that I can't even cry out and anyway, it is too late because she has already fallen to her knees and has bent over me, hugging me, weeping silently. She releases me briefly to wipe some of the blood from my eyes and I wish she had not, because now I can see the man who has hit me, lit by the flames of the burning houses. He is standing behind my friend, and I watch him drop his axe so that he can take his spear in both hands. He lifts it high, pauses for a moment, then drives it down into my friend's back. It goes straight through her and then through me, and we both feel the spear's shaft reverberate as its stone blade splinters on the rocky and now blood-soaked ground beneath us. A small part of me wonders how this pain can be even worse than the pain when the man hit me with his axe, but this doesn't last long because everything is now fading to utter blackness. Yet despite all the screaming, the smell of smoke and blood, and our terror, the last thing that each of us knows is the other's voice, speaking calmly and quite clearly.

"I know this is horrible, but it will soon be over. And we are together now. From now on, we are always together."

Then we both wake up, screaming.

*

We try to carry on as normal, but it is clear after only a few days that this is impossible. Whether we are scraping pelts, roasting hazelnuts, picking berries or trampling hides in tubs of stinking solution, the immediate memory of helpless terror and what feels like endless death is always there. It makes everything else seem so totally pointless that soon we cannot carry out even the simplest of tasks. This is of course noticed almost immediately, first by my mother and then by Serris, so Arlen has no choice but to tell both of them what she and I have been seeing and feeling.

My mother is clearly very distressed by what Arlen tells her but seems to be at a total loss as to what to do about it. Yet Serris, it seems, is not distressed at all. Most people already consider Serris reserved if not rather cold, but even so, the calmness of her reaction causes some surprise. So a few days later, she says to a few people that in her opinion, all any parent can do is help their own children cope with the news of these terrible events in the best way they can, which of course ensures that no one else will say anything about what is happening to Arlen that could be interpreted as a criticism of Serris as her mother. In any case, after a little while, everyone else seems to accept that for whatever reason, Arlen and I are simply that much more sensitive than the other children.

"Why is it just us?" whispers Arlen to me one day in early autumn as we are trying to gather blackberries.

"I don't know."

61

Arlen has asked me this question many times, and each time I have given her the same non-answer.

Finally, we agree that we must speak to at least one of our parents. There is no question of Arlen again trying to raise the subject with her own mother, and somehow, we both know that whatever it was that so troubled my mother in that strange conversation with Gello seems to be troubling her even more now. So that leaves my father, and we agree that Arlen will speak to him about it. My father has in fact always found it easier to talk with Arlen than with me, which is rather odd, given that he is my father and not hers, although it isn't something I've ever really minded.

A week or so later, after my father has returned from the latest hunt, Arlen and I approach him as he is squatting outside our house trying to repair a spear blade. He is so absorbed in this that he does not see us, and for a few minutes, we stand watching him. I recognize the blade he is working on as one of his best ones, large and beautifully carved into an almost perfect shape of a rowan leaf but now missing a large splinter from near the tip. My father is trying to reshape the blade into a smaller one by chipping away small pieces of it with an antler chisel and using a small, round piece of quartzite as a hammer. After a few moments, he puts the antler chisel down and taps very delicately at the blade with the quartzite hammer with, it has to be said, rather indifferent results. He is muttering, and I guess that he is trying to persuade the stone to do what he wants it to do, but it seems that the stone is not listening to him. Yet again, I wonder why my father finds it so hard to admit to himself that he is not a very good flint knapper when it is so obvious to everyone else, including Arlen and me. We have not yet begun flint knapping lessons, but even so, we know enough to realise that my father is about to lose patience, hit the blade far too hard and shatter it. I am hoping very much that he does not do this, partly because I hate seeing him get angry, but mainly because if he does, Arlen won't be able to have the discussion with him that we both need her to have.

She clears her throat to catch my father's attention. He looks up, sees her and smiles. Since Arlen's own father Ulf returned to the All Life, my father has in many ways been a father to Arlen as well. He has without doubt grown very fond of her, and as I mentioned just now, he finds it much easier to speak to her than to me. Arlen says that this is because she reminds him of me, which is true, although not in the way Arlen believes: she is so used to me that she does not yet understand how different I actually am to her and to people like her, including my own parents, and how that differentness can make it so hard for my parents and me to talk to each other.

But for now, my father's smile of pleasure on seeing Arlen is almost immediately replaced by a frown, as though he has guessed what Arlen has come to talk to him about. Yet as she begins to describe what we have been seeing, hearing and feeling, we are both very surprised to see his eyes suddenly fill with tears. He wipes them away and then takes a deep breath, as though bracing himself for the question that he knows is coming.

"Why is this happening to us?" asks Arlen.

She has sat down right next to my father, but because he is such a big man, she has to look almost straight up to talk to him. He doesn't meet her gaze, as though he suddenly finds it awkward to do so. Instead he strokes her hair, affectionately but a little absently. Then his hand drops and his body seems to sag a little.

"Why is this happening to you?" he repeats at last.

For a long time, he is silent again.

"All I can really tell you," he says finally, "is that when I was twelve, my Grandda—the father of my Ma—told me what it feels like to starve."

He pauses again and looks down at Arlen.

"I've never forgotten what he told me. He said that when he was a boy, his whole village began to starve. He didn't know why the food got so very scarce for them back then. None of them knew. But it's what he told me about how it made him feel. Not just hungry all the time, although that was bad enough. It was a feeling he began to have that everyone else had some food. Even though he knew there wasn't any. Then this turned into a feeling that they were keeping this food from him. And then he started to hate them for it, until he hated all of them so much that he wanted to kill them. He ended up hating everyone like this, his Ma and Da, his brothers and sister. Everyone. Later he found out that everyone else felt like this too. Everyone hated everyone else because they were all starving. He told me that if they hadn't found some food when they did, they would have turned on each other. In some other villages, that's exactly what they did."

He sighs again.

"He told me that hating people like that was far worse than just being hungry. And he said he'd do anything rather than feel that way ever again. Or have anyone he cared about feel that way."

He raises his hand as though to stroke Arlen's hair again, but she reaches up and takes his huge hand in both her small ones.

"That's horrible," she says gently, looking at my father. "And I'm really sorry for your Grandda and all those others. But that doesn't make it all right to murder people."

Then Arlen frowns, which means that she's just had an idea. She glances at me, then looks back at my father.

"Or does it?" she asks.

Instead of answering, my father gets to his feet and gestures to Arlen rather brusquely to do the same. Once she is standing, he puts one hand on her shoulder to turn her around so that she is fully facing him and puts his other hand on her other shoulder. He stares down at her gravely.

"Now look here," he says quietly. "I'm probably going to get in trouble with your Ma for telling you this, but I reckon you're old enough to know. I told you what I did about my Grandda just now because things are getting that way for us all again. People are starting to starve, and it looks like some have decided that it's not going to be them. Not just yet, anyway. What's happened—"

He pauses because his eyes have filled with tears again. Frowning, but this time with irritation, he wipes them away.

"What's happened," he continues, "what these people have done to other people—it's horrible, dreadful. Of course it is. So no, of course it isn't all right. Of course there can be no excuse for it. I'm not saying there is. What I am saying is, I can understand it."

I can see that my father knows that Arlen has to ask her next question and that he dreads it even more than her first one.

"And why can Maya and I see and feel these horrible things when no one else can?"

My father shakes his head.

"I don't know. But what I believe is that you and Maya can see and feel things that the rest of us can't because somebody has to. I know it's absolutely horrible for you, but some people, somewhere, have to know what it feels like to be made to suffer. To be made to suffer by other people, I mean. Otherwise, now that some people have decided to kill others so that they won't starve, I don't see how they're ever going to stop."

My father looks intently at Arlen.

"Do you understand?"

She shakes her head.

"No. I'm probably being very stupid, but I don't."

My father sighs. Then he smiles at her, but it's the saddest smile I have ever seen.

"No," he says. "You're not stupid. I can't expect you to understand. But I wonder—"

He stops suddenly.

"I wonder if Maya does," he goes on after a few moments, more to himself than to Arlen. "She is here, I suppose," he says, but without looking around.

Arlen nods.

"Yes," she says. "She's here. But I expect that she won't understand either."

In fact, I did know what my father meant. Not only that, I realised that he was right. But in that different time, when I was so very young, it didn't occur to me to wonder how he could have come to this conclusion. I just assumed that he was doing what he believed was best to try and help Arlen, as her own father would have done if he had still been there. If I'm honest with myself, it's the main reason that I've never been able to forgive him.

A short time after this, there is a night in which Arlen and I do not see any death. Then another, then another, and another after that.

We both know that this means that the Massacres have stopped, although it takes several more weeks before everyone else in the village realises this. When this does finally become clear, someone suggests to the Elders that we should have a feast to celebrate, or as much of a feast as we can make. But then Serris lets it be known that she considers the suggestion deeply inappropriate and that we should be mourning the victims of these appalling acts rather than celebrating the fact that we have not shared their fate. She points out that having a feast would also mean breaking the food quota Laws unless we obtained the prior approval of the Council of the Western Federation which, as she also points out, would never be given. In any case, she adds, the fact that the Massacres have stopped for now is no guarantee that they will not start again. Overall, all food sources are still slowly dwindling, so that each new year will be that much harder than the one before.

And so indeed it proves.

*

I haven't told you about Tallon yet. He's the nearest stream to our village. He really is delightful. He starts at almost the top of the hill and then carries on in a nearly straight line until he joins Verba, and because he goes down over rocks and has no deep pools, his water is fresh almost everywhere. But although we know how lucky we are to have him, the simple act of fetching his water is always frightening, no matter how many times my father assures Arlen that he won't ever let any of us be hurt.

One morning, just after Arlen and I have turned fourteen, my mother loads four leather buckets onto a pole and tells Arlen that she will be going with her. Not so very long ago, all children would have to learn how to carry the buckets like this, empty on the way to Tallon and full on the way back. However, very few children can do this without making any sound amongst the bushes and the lower hanging branches of the trees, and although it is now several years since we learnt of the destruction of the last of the villages in the Southern Federation, making any kind of noise when away from one's village without an armed escort is still regarded as most unwise.

So my mother carries the buckets as she and Arlen move along the path to Tallon as quietly as they can. As usual, I follow silently behind. We are heading to the usual spot where Tallon widens out until his banks are shallow and where it's possible to kneel on the rocks and scoop him out easily. It's only a few hundred paces from the village and the path is a very good one, but when my mother greets the trees, all of whom she of course knows by name, she does so very quietly and without taking her eyes from the way ahead.

It's therefore a huge relief when we are finally standing on Tallon's western bank. My mother fills the buckets, and when she has done so, Arlen and I have to stand silently while she talks to Tallon. As usual I feel that my mother takes far too long doing this. No one would take Tallon's water without thanking him, as that would be both rude and very unwise. You should always say hello to him if you're passing as well, even though there is also the thanksgiving day every Midsummer when we all walk his length and sing to him the song that tells him how grateful we are for all the help he gives to the whole village. But I have never understood why my mother can't just say a polite thank you to Tallon and leave it at that. I don't know exactly what my mother is saying to him because she has made Arlen stand a little way off so that we can't make out her actual words. However, I assume that my mother is asking Tallon if we are all going to be all right, or if some more armed men will come and attack us, or if we will ever have enough food. If she is, this is so silly as to be a little embarrassing. Even I know that if Tallon had any of the answers to these questions, he would have found a way to tell us long before now.

So as my mother is earnestly talking to Tallon, Arlen and I are whispering our own apologies to him and thanking him for being so patient. Then, when my mother has finally finished,

Arlen puts all four filled buckets in a row to load them onto the pole as she simultaneously tries to keep the flies off the water. While all three of us are listening and watching for anything that doesn't feel right, I risk a glance behind her to see if Breccan and Rod are with us, but there is no sign of them.

Arlen and I are also very hungry, although we are both used to that. We're also hot and uncomfortable. But most of all we are afraid. We know that we must look and listen out for men with spears and knives and bows and arrows who might still burst out from the bushes and trees on Tallon's eastern bank and do their best to kill us all. We have done this very many times before, but then I look at my mother and see how afraid she is, and as soon as I realise this, I know what is coming next.

There is the most excruciating pain as an axe smashes down on my head. Blood pours from the huge wound in my scalp, through my hair, down my forehead and into my eyes. I try to wipe the blood away but I can't because suddenly, my hair is pulled hard, jerking my head backwards and nearly breaking my neck. I scream, but almost immediately, my scream turns into a horrible bubbling, choking gurgle as my throat is hacked open. More hot blood gushes from me, some of it splattering onto the rocks and the rest pouring down my neck and soaking into my clothing. I can barely turn my head enough to see Arlen and when I do, she is just standing there staring down at what looks like a big stick in her lower chest. Then I see the man holding the other end of it and I realise it's a spear and I know that Arlen is dying, just like me. I have felt all of these things so many times before, but this time everything is different. Then I realise why. This is not what my mother is afraid of. She is afraid of something much worse. And then, the men, Arlen, my mother, Tallon and everything I have ever known are gone.

*

As I mentioned a little while ago, when first I tried to explain what had happened to me, I said that I had turned into a bird: and that I did so because although it wasn't exactly true, it was the only way I could come close to describing it.

I suppose it's more accurate to say that something happened to me that left me feeling as though I had turned into a bird. I remember standing alone in darkness, which would have been complete except for a single, tiny dot of white light. I remember that this dot of white light looked like a single star between the trees on a moonless night, except that it wasn't above me but straight ahead. I remember feeling the strongest urge to reach this dot of light, and the moment I did, I began to move towards it, very slowly at first but then faster and faster, the dot of light becoming a pool, getting brighter and larger until suddenly, and with an astonishingly powerful sense of coming home, I emerged from the last of the darkness.

Suddenly, I was bathed in the most brilliant sunlight I had ever seen or felt, and I remember that instead of being oppressively bright, it felt wonderfully welcoming. But what I remember most clearly is that wherever I was and however I had got here, I could now see and feel the entire world.

It is the overwhelmingly huge sense of space that first hits me. It is almost like a physical blow, and I know at once that this must be the kind of feeling that the hunters and the wheat gatherers have tried to describe when they speak of being on the Sea of Grass. But I also know that what I am experiencing now is thousands of times more intense. And although this is so different to anything I have ever known before, it feels right. I cannot possibly explain it, but I know as surely as I have ever known anything that this place, wherever and whatever it is, is where I truly belong. The other extraordinarily intense feeling I have, again unlike anything I've ever felt before, is of being so much more alive. As though up to this point, I have been asleep without realising it, and I have finally woken up.

I am above the land and trees, and it feels not as though I am floating but actually flying. For a few moments, all I want to do is spin in the air, glide and swoop, luxuriating in this wonderful feeling, these intense sensations of freedom and vitality. As I do,

I become aware of something so obvious that I can't understand how I could have remained ignorant of it for so long. The world is really in two parts: the land and rivers and trees down below, the place where I have lived up until now, and here—my true home.

After a few moments, it occurs to me to dive down and hover over a small group of houses, which somehow I can see perfectly clearly, despite the thick canopy of leaves. Then I realise with a pleasurable little thrill of surprise that I am looking at my own village. I can see the smoke rising through the roofs of each of the houses, although I can't see anyone moving about. Then I fly upwards again, and this time I decide to follow Verba's valley for a long way until it suddenly narrows and the hills on either side get steeper, closing in on it. Then I turn around and fly back until I am again above Tallon, whom I find without the slightest difficulty. Once again, despite the thick covering of trees, I can somehow see all of him, starting from his spring and then going all the way down until his waters join with those of Verba. Then I dive down again to see if I can find my mother and Arlen. I see my mother standing with her eyes closed and her arms outstretched, talking to Tallon, but I can't see Arlen anywhere. After looking in vain for her for a few moments more, I fly up again and hover, puzzled as to where she could be.

Then I hear the voice.

"It's funny, isn't it?" it says. "Funny how a place can be strange and familiar at the same time."

I know straight away that there is no point in looking to see who has spoken to me. This is not just because I know that there will be nothing to see, but because I feel as though I should already know, even though it is so long since anyone but Arlen, Breccan and Rod has really spoken to me.

"I don't know," I reply, then stop. I am not speaking as I usually do, yet I can clearly hear my own words. This is very disconcerting and makes me feel even more awkward, so I decide that all I can do is formally introduce myself.

"I'm Maya," I say. "Daughter of Frey and Bran, of the Eighth Village in the Western Federation."

"Ah, Maya. Yes. Of course you are. I'm sorry," says the voice.

All at once, the memory of everything from immediately before I found myself here rushes back—I have no idea where it has been until now—and with it comes the sense of helpless panic, obliterating all feelings of shyness and awkwardness.

"The men," I say. "Arlen, my mother—"

The voice interrupts me, urgent yet somehow calm and comforting.

"Arlen and your mother are perfectly all right. Those men, the men that you saw, they—well, they weren't really at Tallon. They were somewhere else and at some time else. And yes, I know that before, both you and Arlen have seen and felt what men like this can do. But this time, Arlen didn't feel or see anything. Only you did. And I know you've never seen anything like that on your own. But it's all right. You will understand soon. You really do not need to worry."

I know straight away that all this is true, and I am hugely relieved.

"Now then, where was I?" says the voice. "Oh yes. I believe I was saying that it's odd that a place can be so familiar and yet every time you go there, it can still take you by surprise."

Although the voice is still soothing, its tone has changed from one of concern and reassurance to a casual, chatty one, which I find very strange. I am also starting to wonder how it knows so much about me and how I am feeling, and I ask my next question before I really mean to.

"I don't mean to be rude or anything, but do I know you? I do, don't I?"

"Ah," says the voice, suddenly sounding awkward itself.

This reply is not what I have been expecting, but I am still far too relieved to know that Arlen and I and my mother are all right and so happy just being where I am, being home, to care very much.

"It's all right," I say, as politely as I can. "You don't have to tell me if you don't want to. It's just that—"

"Just what?" asks the voice quickly.

"It's just that I feel I do," I go on, a little apologetically. "Even though I know I don't."

There's a pause, and when I hear the voice again it still sounds friendly but even more awkward than before.

"It isn't that I don't want to tell you. I do want to tell you. I want to tell you very much. In fact, I need to. It's just that it's, well, a bit difficult right now. You will understand a bit later. I promise you will."

This sounds even odder, but it seems to me I have no choice but to accept it.

"All right," I say. "But can you at least tell me what's happened to me?"

"Well," replies the voice, "now that you're asking me, I have to say I'm not really sure. You see, this has rather taken me by surprise as well. Let me see, now. Oh yes, I know. Do you feel very different?"

I want to say, of course I feel different, you silly voice, I've just turned into a bird! But I stop myself, partly because such a reply would be very ill-mannered but mainly because I know that it wouldn't be true.

"Well, yes, I do feel different," I say at last. "But—"

I don't know how to say what I want to say next, but after a few moments, the voice seems to guess.

"But even though everything's so different, even though you feel so much more alive, you also feel more like you than you've ever felt before?"

I am about to ask the voice how it could possibly know this when it speaks again.

"You want to know how I know." It pauses. "I know because that's exactly how it's always been for me. For all of us, actually."

"All of us?" I repeat quickly. "How many of you are there, then?"

But this time, the voice doesn't answer. I feel very confused by all of this, and I want more than ever to ask the voice exactly who she is—it is a She, I'm certain of that, although that's all I'm certain of—but again, I somehow know that it will do no good.

"Are there other people who come here?" I ask. "Other people like me?"

"Other people like you?" replies the voice, sounding a little surprised. "Oh dear me, no. Well, certainly not now, anyway. Right now, it's just—us."

For a moment I'm worried that the voice sounds faintly reproving, but then I realise that its tone is actually that of sudden resolve, as though up to this point, it hasn't been sure about something but has now made up its mind about it. What is clear however is that I'm going to get no further with this, so I try another question.

"If I'm still me, why am I suddenly so different?"

"Well," says the voice, more comfortably, "are you sure that you know who you were to start with?"

This question seems to make absolutely no sense at all.

"I'm sorry?" I say, as politely as I can. I want to add that I haven't the faintest idea what the voice is talking about, but I don't because again I feel it would be ill-mannered.

"No," says the voice, sounding both rueful and amused. "I don't suppose you do have the faintest idea what I'm talking about. I'll have another go. Now, then, let me see. Ah, I know. Do you feel that you are you?"

It's several moments before I'm able to reply. First, I am still too surprised by the voice apparently hearing what I wanted to say without me actually saying it, and second, the answer to the voice's question is so obvious that I assume that it's the sort of question that no one would ever expect an answer to. But it seems I'm wrong.

"Well?" the voice asks, sounding a little impatient but amused at the same time.

"Of course I feel that I'm me," I say after another few moments. "I'm—well, I'm me."

The voice doesn't answer.

"Aren't I?" I ask, now starting to feel a little worried.

The voice sighs.

"Hmm," it says, again as though speaking to itself, and this time sounding faintly exasperated. "I really had hoped that this time it would be easier. Well, yes, of course you're you," the voice goes on, now clearly speaking to me again. "But what I mean is, how did you come to feel that you're you? How do any of us come to feel that we are who we are?"

The voice pauses again, and this time it doesn't seem to expect an answer, much to my relief.

"I suppose what I mean," the voice continues in a musing kind of way, "is that most of the time we all see ourselves as—as well, just that, I suppose. Ourselves. But isn't that just an idea we have? An idea that, to start with at least, isn't even ours? After all, it's not as though anyone is born with a ready-made idea of who they are and who they're going to turn into as they grow up. Each of us is told who we are by whoever is looking after us: parents, grandparents, uncles, aunts, cousins, Elders. They tell us that our name is so-and-so and that we're their daughter, their grandson, and so on, and we just accept it. Then, as we grow older, we start adding to it ourselves, although we can't really ever take anything away. You can say to yourself, I'm tall, I'm short, I'm not much good at doing this, but I am good at doing that. But you can't suddenly say you're not someone's daughter or someone else's cousin or that your name isn't the one put on you when you were born. But whoever they come from, whether they're from other people or from ourselves, these are all just ideas. And if they're just ideas, can't some of them turn out to be wrong, the way ideas sometimes are? Or, if not wrong exactly, can't they sometimes be replaced by better ideas?"

I still have no idea why the voice is telling me all this or what, if anything, I'm meant to say in answer to it. There is yet another pause, the longest and the most awkward yet.

"Oh dear," says the voice at last. "I've baffled you into silence, haven't I?"

I do a few swoops in the huge cloudless sky. Then I fly back to where I know the voice is patiently waiting for me.

"Who gave you your first idea of who you are, then?" I ask.

The voice laughs, a loud, spontaneous laugh of genuine

surprise and amusement. "Well, you've come to that in a remarkably short time," it says, when its laughter subsides.

I'm more puzzled than ever. I'm also a little offended, as I can see nothing remotely funny in the question I just asked. But again, the voice seems to understand this.

"I'm so sorry," it says. "That must have seemed rather rude of me. But I wasn't laughing at you, really. I was laughing—well, with surprise. Look, it doesn't matter. It'll all be clear soon enough. And anyway, I can tell that there's something else you want to ask me."

I find it a little strange that the voice is prepared to drop the subject so quickly, particularly as it seems to be so very interested in it. I'm also surprised that it seems to know what I'm about to ask, but I'm far too curious not to ask it.

"You said a while ago that you've been here lots of times," I begin, a little hesitantly.

"Yes, that's right," says the voice in an encouraging tone. "I have. Lots of times."

"So you don't actually live here?"

"No," says the voice. "No, I can't truly say that I do. Although sometimes, it feels as though this is my only real home."

It suddenly sounds rather sad and I'm so surprised by this that I fall silent again.

"Oh, never mind me," says the voice. "Go on. Ask your question."

"All right," I say. "Who do you come to visit if nobody actually lives here?"

"Ah."

This time the pause is so long that I'm afraid that despite the voice encouraging me to ask my question, I have somehow offended it by doing so. But when it speaks again, it doesn't sound at all offended, merely uncertain.

"Well," it says slowly, "this is going to sound rather strange. But I've come here to visit you."

This certainly does sound strange. In fact, of all the strange things the voice has said, this is by far the strangest thing yet.

"But I don't understand that either," I protest. "How do you know me at all? And how did you know I'd be here when I didn't know I would be?"

"Oh, no one knew you'd be here," says the voice quickly. "That's why I've had to come visiting here so many times. But on all those other times—all those other visits, and oh dear me, there have been so very many—there was no way of knowing who exactly might be here for me to see. But now that you and I have finally met, it's clear to me that it was you. It was always you, and nobody else. You see—"

The voice stops and sighs as though searching for the right words.

"It was just a matter of time, really," it continues at last. "And patience. Do you see?"

I turn and do a few swoops while I consider this. Then I glide back to where I know the voice is.

"Not really," I reply. "But are you saying that that's why I'm here now? To visit you?"

"Yes," says the voice softly. "Yes, that must be right. Although—"

It hesitates again.

"Although what?"

"You might have come here for other reasons as well," it finishes.

"What other reasons?" I ask, puzzled again.

"Well now," says the voice, resuming its earlier chatty tone, "let's see. Now we're up here, what are you able to do? Something that perhaps you've always felt you needed to do, but haven't been able to before now?"

Again, I want to say, I can fly! But I don't, because somehow, I know that this isn't what the voice means. Then without meaning to, I swoop up over the trees on Tallon's eastern bank, and in another moment, I can see small deer, squirrels, voles, mice, hundreds and hundreds of them, and more birds and insects than I could ever have guessed there were in the entire world. Then I fly back to the village, and in a moment, I am Lind, watching my father glue duck feathers to some arrow shafts; I am Rona, sitting in the sun outside her house with a puppy in her lap; I am Hud, yelling at my son Madoc to stop picking his nose and help me with the mass of nettle fibres I've been trying to untangle for the last two hours; then I am Madoc, feeling angry and resentful at being shouted at by my Da in front of everyone and at the same time a bit ashamed because I know he's right and that I ought to be helping him far more than I do. I turn around again, and in no time, I am back over Tallon. Then I fly upwards to return to the voice.

"I understand," I say.

"I'm sorry," replies the voice with another, but this time very sad sigh. "I do understand how difficult this is for you. But you must know that I cannot help you with this."

The voice is right. I do know.

"But that means I have to go back now," I say dejectedly.

"Yes," says the voice gently. "It does."

"Will I see you again?" I can't help asking. "Well, not see you, I know I can't see you, but—I mean, can I—?"

Suddenly it is my turn to feel awkward, and the voice's turn to help.

"I'm sure we will meet again, Maya. And now we know who you are, I feel that at last—at long last—I'm beginning to understand who I am."

The voice laughs softly. "In fact, it's very clear now," it adds, seemingly more to itself than to me. "It's so obvious. I don't know how I could have been so stupid."

I am too astonished to say anything.

"I'm sorry," the voice continues after a pause. "It isn't really possible to explain any of this just now or why I'm so sure that we will meet again. But I am sure. And it will all be explained by—"

Again, it stops as though searching for the right words.

"Look," it carries on after a moment, "I know I keep saying this, but it really will all become clear to you. Quite soon. I promise."

Suddenly, I remember something else.

"What are the other reasons?"

"I'm sorry?" replies the voice, sounding a little distracted. "The other reasons?"

"You told me that I was mainly the reason you came here," I explain. "So there must be other reasons too. What are they?"

"Well," sighs the voice, this time sounding not just awkward but embarrassed, "you're going to need to know, so I may as well tell you now. It's to see the House of Women. And the House of Men."

I am so stunned by this that I can't reply, as again the voice seems to guess.

"Yes, I do appreciate that that's a bit of a shock," says the voice, sounding so embarrassed that it has dropped to almost a whisper. "But like I said just now, you are going to need to know."

I turn to glide and swoop again, both to recover from my surprise at what the voice has just said but also to luxuriate for the last time in the wonderful sense of freedom.

"Why was I suddenly all those other people?" I ask. "Lind, and Rona, and Madoc and his Da?"

"I'm sorry," says the voice very quickly, sounding slightly perplexed. "Surely we went through that just now. Whose idea is it that you're Maya and not Lind, or Rona, or Madoc or his father?"

"Mine," I reply straight away. "Mine, and theirs."

"Yes," says the voice. "And like all ideas—"

The voice pauses, waiting for me to finish its sentence, which I do.

"Like all ideas, they can be wrong. Or they can change. Replaced by better ideas."

Then something strikes me. Something that seems utterly ridiculous but at the same time completely right.

"I suppose that explains all the animals and birds too," I say. "I could see all of them a little while ago, but I can't see any now."

"Go on," says the voice, sounding amused again.

Now that I am about to explain it, the idea seems even more ridiculous. But then I remember that the voice knows what I want to say, whether I actually say it or not, so I may as well continue.

"Well," I say, "I was going to ask where the animals and birds and insects have all gone. But they haven't gone, have they?"

I hear another soft laugh. "Well done. No, they haven't gone. Quite the contrary. They're all here. Every last one of them in the world."

I am very pleased. But I am also very sad, because I know that my time in this place is over, at least for now. Then one last question occurs to me.

"Why do I need to know what you told me just now? About the—"

This time the voice seems to know not just what I want to say but why I'm unable to say it, so it finishes my question for me.

"About me coming here to visit the House of Women and the House of Men?" it asks briskly, all embarrassment and awkwardness gone. "Because that is the only thing that will convince anyone else that you and I were here at all, of course."

And with that, I am once more standing on Tallon's bank.

*

My mother is still absorbed in her conversation with Tallon, but Arlen is staring at me, so naturally, I have to tell her everything. When I have finished, Arlen glances over her shoulder at my mother, who has finally turned from Tallon and is loading the filled buckets onto the pole.

"We'll have to tell them," I whisper.

Arlen nods, looking utterly miserable. We have both known for a long time that this day would come, but now that it has, we are both still entirely unprepared for it. Arlen hugs me and turns to my mother, who has lashed the end buckets to the pole with heather rope and has picked up the one end of it, expecting Arlen to help her lift it onto her shoulders. But on seeing Arlen's face, she puts the pole down again.

"What is it?" she asks in a rapid whisper. "What did you hear?"

Arlen shakes her head.

"Nothing," she says. "It isn't that."

She takes a very deep breath. She looks up at my mother.

"It's happened," she says.

My mother stares at her blankly.

"Maya," Arlen explains. "It's happened to her at last."

Then she proceeds to tell my mother everything that I have just told her.

*

When Arlen has finished, my mother still says nothing. In fact, for several moments, she gives no sign of having heard anything that Arlen has said. But then she suddenly lunges forward and, leaving the pole and the four brimming buckets to the flies, seizes Arlen by the wrist and half walks, half drags her back to the village.

I follow closely behind, although now and then I have to break into a run to keep up with them. When we arrive in the village, my mother takes Arlen straight to Serris' house. With a shocking disregard of the most basic manners, she simply shoves Arlen before her through Serris' door, so roughly that Arlen misses the drop onto the floor and falls, crying out as her knees hit the hard beaten earth beneath the reeds. Serris is standing by the central fire. To my surprise, she appears neither surprised nor angry at the interruption. Instead, she merely looks expectantly at my mother, who only now seems to be aware of her rudeness.

"Sorry," my mother gasps out. "I'm sorry for bursting in like this. I'm really sorry. But—"

She stops and closes her eyes.

"She saw Maya again," she says simply.

Serris frowns.

"So?" But then suddenly her frown deepens. "You mean—?"

My mother nods.

Serris looks at her for a long time, mouth open, but her face otherwise immobile. Then Serris seems to collect herself and takes a deep breath.

"I see."

She looks back at Arlen. I do too, and although I have known Arlen all my life, it is only now that I realise just how afraid she is of her own mother.

"Come here," Serris says, quietly but firmly.

Together, Arlen and I step over to her. We are now so close that I can smell Serris' sour breath, and as she studies Arlen, I find myself examining all the wrinkles on Serris' face, then watching a solitary louse walk slowly from one white eyebrow to the other.

After looking at Arlen intently like this for at least a minute, Serris suddenly heaves a sigh of exasperation.

"It's no good," she says. "I can't make out a damned thing in here."

Arlen has for a little while been taller than her mother, but Serris turns her around by her shoulder as though she were still a small child. Then, grasping the nape of her neck, she pushes her out through the door of her house and back out into the sunshine. I follow them outside, where I see to my dismay that quite a large crowd has now gathered. Serris glances at a few faces, which is enough to silence the murmuring. In the few moments it takes for her to do so, Arlen turns to me.

"I can't do this," she whispers through clenched teeth.

"Yes you can," I whisper back. "This is what we have waited for. We are so, so close now. We only have to be strong for a little while longer."

I can see that Arlen wants to ask me what I mean, but then Serris, having quietened our audience again with another look, turns back to her.

She reaches out and places her forefinger on Arlen's jaw, turning her head away from me and towards herself.

"It's no good talking to her," she says, mimicking the whispered voice in which Arlen has just spoken to me. "She can't help you right now. Right now, you have to listen to me. You are not in trouble and I am not angry with you. Do you understand?"

Arlen nods. I can tell that she is too scared to speak.

"But you must tell me exactly what happened to Maya just now," Serris goes on. "When she was with you and Frey, getting water from Tallon. Like I just said, I'm not angry with you. But this is very, very important. Do you understand?"

Arlen nods her head then opens her mouth to speak, but no sound comes out. Serris sighs.

"Take some deep breaths."

Arlen does so. One, then a second, then a third.

"That's better," says Serris. "Well?"

"She was with me as usual," says Arlen. "We were just waiting, waiting for her Ma to finish speaking to Tallon. And then Maya saw—"

Arlen looks down again, swallowing hard.

There is something odd in Serris' voice when she speaks again.

"Maya saw it again?" she asks, this time her voice a little hoarse. She swallows. "Maya saw people being murdered by other people?"

There is a gasp from our little audience, although at another glance around from Serris, there is silence again.

Arlen looks up at her mother and nods. Serris glances at my mother who is also watching Arlen very intently, frowning, her face very pale. Then she notices Serris watching her, and she gives a helpless shrug. Serris turns back to Arlen.

"Are you absolutely sure?"

"Yes," says Arlen, nodding again. "Except this time—"

She stops and bites her lip. I put my hand on her shoulder.

"Except this time what?" asks Serris.

"Except this time, she said it was different. It was us. Not other people being killed, but us. Maya and me, I mean. Maya saw these men, and one of them pulled her hair and killed her with his knife. Then before she died, she saw that another of the men had pushed his spear right into me, and she saw me looking down at it sticking into me. She knew that I knew I was dying, and that as I died, I was looking around for her, and she wasn't there any more. But I didn't see any of this. Only Maya saw it."

Arlen realises she has started to gabble.

She stops and takes another deep breath.

"She'd left me and become like some kind of bird," she says, more slowly. "Anyway, she was flying, high up in the sky. When she came back, she told me."

Arlen stops again, and I can tell that, like me, she is expecting Serris either to slap her or to laugh. Serris does neither but continues to stare into her daughter's face.

"Are you absolutely sure?" asks Serris again.

"Yes," Arlen replies.

"How did Maya become a bird? Or whatever it was she did become?"

"I don't know," replies Arlen, shrugging helplessly. "She doesn't know either. I'm sorry," she adds.

Serris says nothing for quite a long time. When she speaks again, she does so very suddenly, so that both Arlen and I jump in surprise.

"What were you both doing just before this happened? Just before Maya saw the men come?"

Arlen glances at my mother apprehensively. Serris looks at my mother as well, and she, returning Serris' look, blinks slowly and very slightly inclines her head towards her. Watching them, I suddenly know that somehow, they have spoken to one another without actually saying anything out loud.

"Whatever happens," Serris has told my mother, "and whatever I do or say, you must not interrupt."

"Don't worry," my mother has replied in the same way, "I won't. I trust you."

It is not the sudden evidence of how very close Serris and my mother are that disturbs me, so much as the fact that I have never noticed this before. Serris turns back to Arlen, eyebrows raised.

"Well?"

Arlen looks round at me, anxious.

Serris notices and heaves a short and impatient sigh.

"Go on, tell her," I whisper to Arlen. "It's all right."

Arlen gives me a weak smile then looks back at Serris.

"Maya was saying sorry to Tallon for her Ma talking to him

for so long," she says. "Then Maya went quiet for quite a long time. When I looked for her again, she wasn't there any more." She drops her gaze, swallowing. "She says that's when she saw the men come and kill her and me. But like I just said, this time, only she saw it. I didn't see anything at all. And then she became a bird. Or whatever it was she became."

Serris continues to stare at her daughter's face as though searching for something. Her brows are contracted, and her lips are moving slightly, as though she is having great difficulty following what Arlen is telling her.

"This time it was just Maya who saw you and her being killed, as you were standing with her and Frey?" she asks finally. "By Tallon, just now?"

Arlen nods. There is another long pause before Serris asks her next question.

"Did Maya become a bird to get away from the men?"

"No," says Arlen quickly. "No, she didn't want to become a bird or anything like that. One of the men killed her and she just—"

Arlen stops, then shrugs again.

"She just did," she finishes.

Serris nods slowly. Then something seems to strike her.

"Has Maya ever talked to you before about becoming a bird?"

"No," replies Arlen, as surprised by the question as I am.

I am beginning to be afraid that having so many people see her make consistently wrong guesses will make Serris angry. But then I see that just at this moment, she has forgotten everyone except Arlen and me. She looks down for a few seconds, frowning. Then she looks up at Arlen again.

"Did Maya say how it felt? Being like a bird in the sky?"

"Yes," says Arlen immediately. "She said it felt really good. That it felt right. As though she was coming home."

Serris nods again. Then she takes a deep breath and closes her eyes as though plucking up enough courage to ask a question the answer to which she is afraid to hear.

"And did Maya speak to anyone when she was in the sky?"

"Yes. Someone spoke to her, someone who was already there. Maya said that she doesn't know who this person was. But Maya also said—"

Arlen gasps suddenly and looks round at me with an expression of pain and surprise. For a moment I stare back at her blankly, but then I look down to see my hand gripping her upper arm tightly. I release her, leaving four red welts across her skin.

"She said what?" asks Serris.

"It's all right," I whisper to Arlen. "Tell her."

Arlen shuts her eyes.

"The person that spoke to Maya in the sky told her that she was there to meet her. But this person also told Maya that she—this person who spoke to Maya in the sky, I mean—goes there to visit the House of Women and the House of Men."

There are gasps of shock from our little audience and Serris flinches slightly as though she has just been stung by a nettle. Then she looks briefly at my mother, who is simply staring at Arlen. She turns back to her daughter.

"How do you know Maya isn't lying to you?" she demands. "For that matter, how do I know you're not lying to me?"

Arlen is clearly at a loss as to how to answer these questions. She shakes her head.

"I'm not lying," she says at last. "And I know Maya isn't lying. She couldn't lie to me, not ever."

Serris smiles at Arlen.

She reaches out and gently strokes her hair, twining it amongst her fingers in what no doubt looks to some as the most loving and motherly of gestures. But I can see, and Arlen can feel, that with one good twist, she can rip out the entire handful. She leans close to Arlen so that their noses are almost touching.

"I know you don't believe that Maya could ever lie to you," whispers Serris, so quietly that only Arlen and I can hear her. "But maybe one day you'll discover things she might have told you but chose not to. So what if I'm right about that, and you're wrong?"

I have so far managed to stand by and watch all of this

without intervening, but suddenly this is no longer possible. I close my eyes for a moment and when I open them again, it is I who am staring right into Serris' face, and it is my hair Serris is gripping. Serris' face goes slack with shock, and I know she has recognized Me.

"How dare you?" I whisper to her, so quietly that only she can hear me. "How dare you—you, of all people—question Me? Have you forgotten that I made you what you are? Does the thing made dare ask questions of the One who made it?"

Serris is still too shocked to say anything and simply stares back at Me. I reach up and, taking her hand in both of Mine, pull it from My hair. She makes no attempt to resist.

"You have always known this day would come," I go on. "You have pretended to yourself that you haven't, but you have. I told you on the day that you gave Me your oath. Do you dare behave as though I have released you from it?"

I want to keep on studying Serris' face, to see how she is going to react. But I cannot help shutting my eyes again, and when I open them once more, I am back at Arlen's side, looking at Serris as she stands totally still, staring at her daughter.

"Go on," I whisper to Arlen. She nods.

"So do you understand now, mother?" she says. "Do you see why we cannot be lying?"

*

Once, or so the old stories go, no one could be considered to have become an adult until they had been taken to the House of Women or the House of Men. But that would have been in a different time, so even if those old stories are true, no one now knows why this would have been so.

In fact, no one even knows why the House of Women and the House of Men are even called that, particularly when they're not houses at all and clearly never were. Instead, they are simply huge sandstone rocks about two hundred paces from one another, simply sticking up out of the ground, on the summit of a large hill just under four days east of our village. Each is covered in very beautiful but strange and rather disturbing-looking carvings, and it used to be said that these carvings were made in an attempt to make the stones resemble the huge houses in which the Lost Ones lived in their bizarre treeless wasteland. But the discouragement of any kind of speculation about the Lost Ones is enough to ensure that no one enquires further about who made these carvings or why, or what exactly they were meant to depict. All that can be said with any real certainty is that they too were made in a very distant time.

Both the House of Women and the House of Men are reasonably close to the main trade route between the Southern, Eastern and Northern Federations, so plenty of people have seen them, some many times. But no one dares go any closer to them, not even to admire the ancient carvings. Touching them is absolutely forbidden by Law, and everyone knows that, unlike some Laws, this one is strictly enforced.

Sooner or later, from someone or another but usually from their parents, every child learns about the Two Boys. The Two Boys lived in a village in the Eastern Federation, near to the House of Women and the House of Men. Instead of learning how to become good and useful members of their village, they were usually up to some prank or another. Whenever they were caught, they were of course punished, but unfortunately, they were the kind of boys whom punishment seems to make more determined than ever to misbehave. So the Two Boys got up to more and more mischief, until one day, they decided that they were going to go to the House of Men and climb up onto it. Unluckily for them, someone overheard them making their plans. They alerted the village Elders, who concluded that the matter was so serious that they had no alternative but to inform the nearest Law Sayer. What advice the Law Sayer gave became clear when a few nights later the Two Boys duly sneaked out of their houses to commit their crime and were followed all the way by three of their village's best archers. The Two Boys had every chance to turn back, but it seems that they were bent on their wickedness. Finally, they arrived at the House of Men, and even then, it would not have been too late. But the Two Boys then did what they, along with everyone else, had been told time and time again should never, ever be done and placed their hands on the actual rock. The moment they did so, the archers loosed the arrows that had been aimed at them in the moonlight.

They had aimed to cripple only, not to kill, and the Two Boys, all bravado now completely gone, crying out for their mothers and begging for forgiveness in between their screams of agony, were taken back to their village. There, before everyone, including their weeping parents, they were flayed alive. The bodies were dismembered and the meat, the brains and the guts all fed to the village dogs. Then, instead of being taken to their village Station, the bones were just burnt, like so much old rubbish, and the fragments that were left were buried amongst the trees. The skins were taken back to the House of Women and the House of Men and pegged out, one in front of each, to serve as a warning.

Those skins have long since dried up and blown away, but by then, the story itself had become the warning, and it has been a very effective one ever since. This is because, terrible as what happened to the Two Boys is, what disturbs every child most on being told about them is that when they ask the names of the Two Boys, the reply is that nobody knows. The Two Boys had tried to do something so wicked that they had been destroyed more thoroughly than anyone before or since, and so were gone forever, like fires that had been stamped out and then doused in filthy water. They would forever be remembered only as the Two Boys, the would-be perpetrators of a vile crime, their names, along with all they ever were and all they would ever have been, totally obliterated.

*

Arlen and I are therefore well aware that what we have told Serris about the House of Men and the House of Women is going to make things rather difficult for a little while. But we are not prepared for what Serris does only a week later, which is to ask Rona if she will take us with her on the wheat-gathering expedition that she is preparing to take out the following month.

Rona is so surprised that she drops the scraper with which she has been preparing the hide stretched out in front of her house and sits back on her haunches, staring at Serris with her mouth open.

"You want us to take a child with us?" she finally asks, incredulous.

"Two children, actually," replies Serris. "As you know, wherever Arlen goes, Maya goes too. Although of course Maya doesn't take much looking after. And they're not exactly children," she adds. "They are fourteen."

Rona ignores this.

"Why?" she demands.

"Well," says Serris equably, "they have to learn, don't they?"

Serris is deliberately avoiding the point, and I can see that Rona has absolutely no intention of letting her do so.

"They learn when they're strong enough to walk for a whole day without whining," she snaps back. "When they can find their own food and ration it for themselves for as long as we're away. When they know what to do when someone else in the group faints or screams or starts puking their insides out. When they've learnt what they need to know so that they can bring back more food than they set out with."

Although Rona is rather squat and looks a bit clumsy, she is actually very agile, and in what looks like one flowing movement, she has stood up and stepped over to Serris.

"When they're an asset to everyone else in the party," she hisses straight into Serris' face. "Not a damned liability."

Serris continues to smile pleasantly, as though Rona has just politely wished her good morning. Then she looks at Arlen.

"But these two aren't just any two fourteen-year-olds, are they? Oh, I'm sorry, I'm forgetting. You were away when it happened, weren't you? So perhaps you hadn't heard?"

Slowly, Rona's scowl is replaced by a broad grin.

"Oh, I heard all right," she says, with unmistakeable malice. "Everyone's heard all about it. Don't you worry."

Arlen glances at me, nervous. Like me, she is expecting Serris to be angry at Rona's goading, but instead, her pleasant smile only widens, and she shrugs. Rona's grin vanishes and her truculent expression returns.

"Anyway, I don't see what difference that makes."

Serris shrugs again. "Neither do I," she says lightly. "But of course, that's not to say it won't make a difference. Who knows?"

She touches Arlen's hand and turns back to her house, but then she looks back at Rona, who scowls at her once again.

"Oh, just one other thing," Serris says, even more casually than before. "Arlen ought to be the gathering party's Fire-Keeper. Wouldn't you say?"

Angry as Rona is, she is so astonished by this that once again, she can only gape at Serris.

Arlen and I of course know how to make and keep fire, this being an essential part of every child's secondary education. No matter how many times your bow drill, block and tinder, or the goatskin bag holding them have to be replaced, your fire kit is somehow always the same one that you proudly received as a small child, and the fire you make from it for yourself is also yours, a gift to you from the All Life, to use for your benefit as you see fit. However, the acting Fire-Keeper on any hunt or gathering party carries the Village Fire, through which we all remain connected with one another, no matter where we happen to be. It is therefore easily the most important role in any hunt or foraging party, far more important even than that of the leader.

"What did you just say?" Rona finally manages to gasp out.

"I said," replies Serris in the same light tone, "that presumably you agree with me that Arlen should be Fire-Keeper for your wheat gathering party."

Rona closes her eyes and puts both her hands to her head as though something has gone wrong with it. She is silent for several long moments. "I'm sorry," she says finally, eyes still shut. "I don't follow you. Why would I agree with that?"

"Because," says Serris, in the kind of patient manner that someone else might use when speaking to an eager and well-meaning but rather slow-witted child, "as Fire-Keeper, Arlen connects us all. She's connected to Maya, and now it seems that Maya is somehow connected to this person she met in the sky a few days ago. And since this person, whoever she is, seems to know a few things worth knowing, I'd say that a chance for us all to connect with her is one well worth taking. Wouldn't you?"

Rona stares at her for another long moment. Then without another word, Serris takes Arlen's hand, turns and walks back to her house. For a moment I am uncertain as to whether to follow them there, but then Arlen gives me a pleading look, so I do. Arlen stoops and goes through the doorway, but just before Serris does the same, she turns to me.

"I know this is what you want," she says, the pleasant tone she has been using with Rona now completely absent. "So I hope it's worth it."

Serris speaks to me only very rarely, and when she does, she can never quite keep the bitterness out of her voice. But to be fair, she always did understand me quite well.

This is indeed what I want.

*

I did of course realise by this time that everything was beginning to change forever, but strangely, I didn't find myself wishing that it wasn't.

I try to explain this a few days later to my brothers Breccan and Rod, as the three of us watch our mother teaching Edra to find edible roots without trying to eat whatever else she finds. Our mother is nearly seven months pregnant with her fifth child, and it seems that looking after our increasingly active little sister is proving a lot more difficult than she had expected.

"But surely that would've been easier," says Breccan reasonably. "If this wasn't happening, I mean. You'd be spared all this shit—"

He stops at the warning look I give him, then grins. "All this nonsense," he concludes with unnecessary deliberation.

"Yes, of course it would," I reply. "I know that. But that's a bit like saying it'd be easier if I wasn't me. Do you understand?"

"Not in the slightest," says Breccan, beaming at me.

"Me neither," says Rod.

I frown at them.

"What I mean is that this is me," I explain, trying to keep the irritation out of my voice. "This is what I am. All of what I am."

"Is it?" asks Rod, his broad smile suddenly replaced with a puzzled frown. "Don't you mean it's the other way around? That all of you is part of It? Whatever It is?"

He's right. I nod slowly.

Rod seems about to say something else but then stops himself. Instead, he gives me a rather tight-lipped, awkward smile and puts one hairy forearm across my shoulders. I know that physical gestures of affection always make Rod feel a little self-conscious, as indeed they do me, but I still like it when he makes them, especially when they're so unexpected.

"It's how it's always been for all three of us, hasn't it?" he says quietly. "Well, ever since—you know—" His voice trails off, knowing he doesn't need to explain any further. Suddenly, he takes his arm from my shoulders and points past our mother.

"Oh dear," he says, laughing.

Our mother glances up from the honeysuckle twine she has been plaiting just in time to see Edra about to try her new teeth out on a long, wriggling earthworm. She quickly gets to her feet and steps over to Edra, grabbing the chubby little wrist and taking the worm from her. After whining briefly in protest, Edra seems to forget about the worm and resumes stabbing at the ground with her miniature digging stick. The three of us stand watching in silence for a while, then Breccan speaks again.

"Maya?"

The different tone in his voice makes me look up sharply.

"What?"

"Is it going to happen again?"

I nod firmly.

"Oh yes. Yes, it is. I don't know how, or when, or whether it'll happen to Arlen, or to me, or to both of us at the same time. But it is going to happen again. In fact, it'll keep on happening until—"

I can't finish, and I shrug helplessly.

"Sorry," I whisper.

Breccan and Rod have been looking at me closely. Then they exchange glances.

"I see," says Rod finally. "Like that, is it?"

I nod slowly again.

"How come you're so sure?" asks Breccan.

"I don't know," I reply, shrugging again. "I just am."

Rod frowns at me.

"Hmm. You might need to work a bit on that, you know."

I am just about to ask him what he means when our mother's name is called, and it's time for me to go. I turn away, but Breccan puts his hand out to stop me.

"One more thing," he says, voice lowered. "Gorn."

"What about him?" I ask, rather puzzled by the abrupt change of subject. Rod leans forward, his voice also lowered.

"This thing that's happened, or is happening, to you and Arlen. He really doesn't like it."

"I don't care," I reply, in what I hope is a casual way. "I really don't like him."

Rod frowns, clearly feeling a little awkward.

"Yes, well, nobody does. But we've—erm—" He glances at Breccan, who is nodding at him encouragingly, then looks back at me. "Well, we've seen the way he's been looking at Arlen these last few days."

"I can't help that," I reply, a little defensively. In fact, I have noticed the way that a lot of boys, including Gorn, have been looking at Arlen lately.

Breccan frowns.

"No, I know you can't. Look, all we're saying is, watch out for him."

Breccan and Rod are hardly ever serious when talking to me, so I can always recognise those rare occasions when they are.

"All right," I say. "Will you two be around for a while?" I add, eager to change the subject. "To help Ma, I mean?"

Breccan and Rod exchange glances again, and when they both look back at me, their smiles aren't the usual ones that mean that they're about to make fun of me, but ones of genuine affection and warmth. I am so unprepared for this that I feel myself blushing and I have to look away.

"Of course we'll be around," says Rod softly. "It's why we're still here."

He nods at Breccan. "Well, it's why the two of us are still here, anyway."

*

A couple of weeks later, Arlen and I go to find Torban. Being nearly forty years old, Torban has not ventured far from the village for many years, but once, he was one of the ablest hunters on the Sea of Grass in the entire Western Federation. This is why no one can join either a hunting party or a wheat-gathering expedition until Torban is satisfied that they have learnt enough to do so properly. If he is a little surprised at being presented with Arlen and me as his latest pupils, he does not show it and we join his class comprising the sixteen-year-olds who are there to learn not just how to survive on the Sea of Grass for up to an entire month, but how to help every other member of their group to do the same.

From Torban, we learn about the ways in which being on the Sea of Grass is so very different from the life we know amidst the trees. He teaches us how to stop ourselves staring into the open sky even though we somehow want to, but always to make sure our eyes stay on the person we're talking to or on the ground ahead of us, or at some fixed point in the distance to which we're heading.

We practice keeping our eyes shaded until they can adapt to the endless glare of the unbroken sun. Torban explains how to find fresh water and how always to pitch camp on a south-facing slope, because that will hold the sun's heat longest. He tells us what plants we will find on the Sea of Grass, which ones we can eat, and which ones can be used for medicines and to treat wounds. Torban even tells us how to walk slowly so that we don't become exhausted and how always to take even strides so that we don't end up walking around in a big circle. Above all, he tells us how to see the sky, particularly on a cloudless night, without beginning to scream in terror.

For this, the last and by far the most important lesson, Torban makes us all stand up and put our arms tight around one another until we have formed a tightly bound little huddle. Then he walks around us several times, first one way, then the other, examining us as though looking for something. We are all feeling self-conscious and a little silly. Then Gorn sniggers.

Gorn is eighteen, and as I have already reminded Breccan and Rod, I really don't like him. I am far from alone in this, as Gorn is easily the most disliked person in the entire village. He was never particularly pleasant or endearing when he was younger, but he is particularly unpopular now. It had been rumoured for some time that Gorn's main interest was watching the younger girls in the village when he believed that there was no one around to see him doing it. But there was nothing that could be formally reported to the Elders until just over three years earlier when he tried to touch Mira. Mira, who was only ten at the time, had been mending some clothes alone in her house. Mira squirmed away from Gorn, and when he tried to grab her again, she stabbed him right through his foot with the large antler needle she'd been using. Gorn howled, and Mira's father Lodin came running. As soon as Mira told her father what had happened, Lodin put his own foot over Gorn's wounded one to hold it down and, ignoring Gorn's protests that he hadn't done anything wrong and that Mira had made everything up, rammed his spear right through it, splintering all the major bones.

Mira's account of what Gorn had tried to do to her, Lodin crippling Gorn and in doing so breaking the large spear blade that had cost some of the village's finest tanned hides all meant that the matter had to be referred to the village Elders. They dismissed Gorn's repeated protestations of innocence and found that the actions of Lodin were entirely justified. Lodin, incidentally, was quite unrepentant anyway, remarking that it was worth ruining one of our village's most valuable spearpoints just to hear Gorn scream.

Since then, Gorn has had to use a stick to get about and it has taken him nearly two years to do that well enough to be considered for one of the wheat-gathering parties when otherwise he would have been eligible at sixteen. The fact that he will never again be able to run means that joining a hunting party is out of the question, and although Gorn's father, Mekill, has never complained about this—he's actually a very nice man and doesn't seem to like his son any better than anyone else—his mother Ina has always gone on to anyone prepared to listen about how Lodin's impetuous action has deprived the village of another hunter when they are needed more than ever and how this therefore ought to be reported to the Law Sayers. However, as the village Elders had pronounced on the matter, that was the end of it. And as Lodin said, what had happened with Mira showed that Gorn would never have made a decent hunter anyway, which everyone finds rather amusing, except, of course, for Gorn and Ina.

Since Gorn has never been the kind of person to see that he had brought all this on himself, it has made him sourer than ever, and as Breccan and Rod have reminded me, he now seems to have a particular issue with Arlen. He has never tried to touch her, as apart from his experience with Mira, he is far too afraid of Serris. All he has ever done therefore is glower at Arlen, but this does seem to have intensified since what happened on Tallon's bank became the talk of all the Federations.

Another way in which Gorn attempts to make himself feel better is by always trying to give everyone the impression that just about everything is faintly absurd or somehow beneath him, but in ways that only he is clever enough to see. Not surprisingly, this only makes him more disliked than ever. So, when in response to what Torban has just said, Gorn sniggers in his usual condescending way, the rest of us in the class are rather surprised to see Torban smile.

"Come over here, son," he says to Gorn, beckoning jovially.

With a broad grin, Gorn takes his arms from around Suma and Finn and takes a step towards Torban. The moment he does so, Torban suddenly shoulder-charges him, hitting him so hard that Gorn goes crashing to the ground, yelling in pain. Torban regards him briefly and then sighs as though mildly disappointed. He turns back to the rest of us.

"Now there you are, you see," he says. "If I hit any of you like that, you wouldn't fall. Because you're supporting one another. And that's what you're going to have to do when you get out there. Because out there, you can expect a damn sight more than just the risk of falling on your arse."

Without taking his eyes from us, Torban reaches down with one hand, grips Gorn by his upper arm and twists it upwards so that to prevent it from being dislocated, Gorn has to scramble back upright as quickly as his crippled foot will allow.

"Once you're out there," Torban continues, letting go of Gorn with a look of distaste and dusting his hands ostentatiously, "you're going to be afraid. How do I know that? Because everyone is. You're going to be dazzled by the sunlight, obviously, although you'll find your eyes get used to that pretty quickly. You'll be hit by the wind, which isn't too bad to start with until you realise that it isn't ever going to stop. But it's the space that'll really get you. You'll feel as though you're going to get sucked into the big blue emptiness. Your throat will start to close up, so you can't breathe properly. You might lose all sense of direction, perhaps even your balance. You might sweat, shake, or feel like you want to throw up. Some of you will throw up. But that's not the worst of it. That'll come at night, because that's when you'll see the stars. Not the stars like you've seen them before, a few dots of friendly white light peeking through the branches and the leaves. Because where you're going, there aren't any branches and leaves. Instead, up there, at night, there's nothing but the stars. More than you could ever count, even if you spent the rest of your life trying to do it. Some of them even move, shooting across the blackness like an arrow."

He shrugs.

"There's no point in me trying to tell you what it feels like, because everyone has to see it and feel it for themselves. So I can't tell you what it's like to look at them and feel like you're going mad. All I can tell you is that it's happened to me, just like it's happened to all the hunters, all the wheat-gatherers. Anyone who's ever been on the Sea of Grass who tells you different is lying."

Torban pauses again as though waiting for some kind of answer, but none of us knows what to say.

"Many of you, probably all of you, are going to feel this kind of fear," he goes on. "More afraid than you've ever felt before. You might even feel that you're going to die. But you won't. What you'll feel isn't much fun, but it can't kill you. And you can learn to control it."

He glances at Gorn, who is still brushing the dirt from his backside, then jerks his head towards us. Gorn rejoins our group, and with a gesture from Torban, we tighten our holds on one another. Torban nods approvingly.

"And this is how," he says. "By knowing and remembering what this feels like. What it feels like to be as close to each other as this. By knowing that when you're like this, nothing can hurt you. By making sure that you're never more than ten paces from at least two other people and, when any one of you feels afraid, you say that. You say, 'I'm afraid,' as loud as you can. And at least two of those nearest to you will come and hold you like you're holding each other now. Until you're a bit less afraid than you were before, and you feel that you can go on. And that's what we're going to practice now."

So, we practice helping one another for the rest of that day. The next day, we will make our final preparations and we will depart the day after that.

However, that night, after Arlen and I have gone to sleep, I see something I've never seen before.

I am woken up by someone shaking my shoulder. For a few moments I try my hardest to ignore this, not so much because I want to stay asleep, warm under a pile of deerskin blankets, but because I know why I am being woken up.

My shoulder is shaken again, harder this time. Very reluctantly, I push the blankets from me and sit up, the sudden rush of cold air on my face startling me into full wakefulness. I run my tongue around my teeth to see if any more have come loose in the night, and I sigh with relief at finding that none have. Then I put my hands through my hair, and again to my relief, rather less of it than usual comes away in my fingers.

I look at the man who has been shaking my shoulder. He is not Bran, but I know he is my father. Briefly, I wonder why my father and not my mother has woken me, but then I hear a woman's voice. I look round and in the dim light of the oil lamps I see two younger children, a boy and a girl, sitting in their own piles of deerskin blankets and watching me. Their faces are so thin that their eyes seem abnormally large. I know that they are my younger brother and sister. A woman who is not Frey but whom I know to be our mother is speaking soothingly to them both. She is telling them that although they will not see me, their sister, for a long time, I will return to them all one day. I know that my brother and sister, both of whom are trying very hard not to cry, do not understand what this woman—our mother—is telling them and are therefore not in the least comforted by it. Yet I also know that my mother is right.

I climb out of my bed. Aside from having to put on a second hooded cloak and some mittens, I don't need to dress because, like everyone else, I have been stitched into my winter clothing since the fresh snows began in early autumn. My mother pushes back the heavy deerskin tent flaps and stands back to let me step through. A moment later, I am outside my family's tent where a small group has already gathered. It is very cold, but then none of us have ever known a time when it was not, and we stand in the deep snow waiting for some others to join us. It is too dark for me to see them, but I can tell from the sounds they make—no actual speech, just whimpers and the occasional sob, hastily choked back—that they are the four girls of roughly my age from the six families that make up our clan. Then, without a word, we are led away from the houses into the blackness.

For a long time, all I can hear is the wind, the soft crump of our own footsteps in the fresh snow and some muffled sobbing, sniffling and wailing. But then suddenly, a low, monotonous humming begins, which slowly gets louder and louder. After a few moments, I can make out that it is several human voices, but I cannot tell whose they are, nor whether they are close or a very long way away.

Even though it is dark, I know where the path that leads straight up the hill to the House of Women is, so I also know right away that we are not on it. Instead, we are being led along the flat ground west of the village. We walk along this path for a long time, accompanied by the strange continuous humming, ignoring several other paths through the snow, all heading south, up the hill.

The path we are on leads straight into a copse of birches, none of which are significantly taller than a man. I have a dim recollection of seeing this copse before, but only from a distance. Yet I know that I have never entered it, which means that this must be the furthest west I have ever been. Then the girl who for the last two hours has been walking just in front of me gasps and stops so suddenly that I blunder right into her. I look up to see what has made the girl stop, a flickering light moving ahead amongst the stunted trees. The humming stops too, but then I am shoved hard in the back and a woman whose voice I have never heard before hisses at me.

"Shut up, you. And keep moving."

I desperately want to say that it wasn't me that gasped, but I am too afraid to speak. Then everyone starts walking again. The humming resumes, but this time it's somehow different, and as we get closer to the strange light moving up ahead, I see that it's a torch. As we get closer still, I see that it is held by another woman I don't know, with dozens of girls cowering behind her. I don't see any more because as soon as she sees the group approaching her, this woman thrusts the torch down into the snow to put it out. The two groups merge, the humming now louder than ever.

This larger group carries on walking in almost complete darkness for what seems like several hours. I am finding it very hard to keep track of time, impossible to keep any sense of direction and the pains in my knees and hips that come whenever I walk for more than an hour or two are now so intense that I have to bite my lip to stop myself from crying out. We meet another three groups of girls led by women with torches, and each time the humming stops just long enough for this new smaller group to join our larger one before it begins again. Finally, the group turns south and starts to head up the hill.

After a while, we reach another, much larger group of birches, so much larger than the first as to be almost a small woodland. But we only walk through it for a short time before these trees, too, begin to thin out so that I can once again see the cloudy night sky. Then it is my turn to gasp because the sky here is the wrong colour. Instead of dark grey, it's a strange, dirty yellow.

Then there are no more trees at all, and I can see why the night sky has changed colour. Although I know that I am meant to stay silent, I cannot help gasping again, because ahead are the two biggest fires that I have ever seen. Huge flashes of flame appear, then vanish, then appear again whilst thousands and thousands of shining cinders are flying upwards into the still air. We are still a good fifty paces or so away from these fires, but already we can feel their heat and are reluctant to go any closer. Then I hear the same woman's voice from what seems like a very long time ago.

"Move. You've got to keep moving."

As we start shuffling forward again, I look for the House of Women. I can't see it, and for a moment, I am confused until I see that this is because it is hidden by a crowd. It is the largest group of people I have ever seen, and it is composed entirely of women: the clouds of condensation arising from it are almost as big as the clouds of smoke coming from the fires. For several moments, it seems as though all these women are staring at us as we look apprehensively back at them. Then, as though a signal has been given, this group moves quite quickly to form two lines of roughly equal length stretching out towards the new arrivals from each side of the House of Women. There is yet another gasp. The carvings on the House of Women, lit up by the two fires, have been picked out in some very bright colours, although even with the glare of the flames, it is still not light enough to see what the colours actually are. In between these carvings, there are hundreds of figures, apparently human, again brilliantly painted in some bright colours. The continual flaring of the flames makes it look as though the figures are moving, and although from this distance they appear to be little more than sticks, I realise as I get closer to them that they have in fact been depicted very skilfully so as to suggest a huge number of people rushing around in panic in the midst of some enormous, complicated structures.

I know that these beautiful but strange and rather disturbing-looking pictures and carvings are very famous, but I can't remember why. I look at them, trying very hard to recall where I have seen them before. But then there is yet another loud collective gasp and a few cries, all swiftly silenced. I look up to see a figure standing on top of the House of Women. I can tell that it is a woman, her arms held up and her legs spread wide, but for several moments I am confused because there is something wrong with this woman's face. Then I realise what it is, and why more and more girls are starting to scream. Where the eyes and nose should be, there are black holes, separated from one another by a dark smoothness: the woman's face is not a face at all, but the upper front part of an ancient human skull.

A girl immediately to my left collapses into the soft snow with a quiet moan. I turn to see who it is, but before I can, two women have darted towards the slumped figure, seized her and have begun to drag her away through the deep drifts. I want very much to see where they are taking her, but then my right arm is tugged hard.

"You. Come with me. Now."

Yet another woman I don't know pulls me away from the long line that now stretches back from the House of Women.

"What is it? What did I do?" I whisper in a panicky voice.

"Shut up," hisses the woman, gripping my arm still tighter.

"Are you going to kill me?"

"No, but I'll punch you in the face if you don't shut up. Now come on."

I am pulled away from the House of Women for twenty paces or so. It's hard to walk, not because of the deep snow but because my legs are now shaking so much. I am concentrating very hard on not stumbling so that it is several moments before I see that instead of getting lighter—dawn can't be far off now—it's actually getting darker. The light from the huge fires is being suppressed, although I can't see how because of the lines of women in front of my captor and me. But then a glow appears around the House of Women itself, and for a moment I assume that it is the sun finally coming up before realising that it must be coming from a third fire directly behind it. My captor pulls my arm hard again.

"Right. Now shut your eyes and don't speak."

"What?"

The woman steps around in front of me and draws her hand back to hit me, but before her blow can land, I shut my eyes and then everything is in bright light. All at once, night has suddenly turned into day so that now I can see not only the House of Women but the House of Men as well. It too has two huge fires burning either side of it and a third one behind, and two lines of roughly equal length stretching back from it, although these lines comprise boys, being herded by a group of men. Then, as I watch, the House of Men and the House of Women themselves begin to move. Incredibly, the two rock outcrops are moving towards one another, very slowly at first, but then faster and faster until it seems they are going to collide. But then, instead of colliding, they just slowly merge into one another until there is only one outcrop upon which the terrifying figure is still standing.

"Do you know Her?"

Although it has been so long, I am not in the least surprised to hear the voice again.

"Yes," I whisper.

"Do you really?" says the voice, sounding rather distant and almost amused. "We will see. Listen."

The Skull-Faced Woman begins to declaim.

"Before the beginning of all things, in the space before space and in the time before time, there was the All Life. The All Life did not know it was the All Life, as it was not called that, there being nothing else anywhere to call it anything. It simply was. And it was the only thing that was.

"The All Life knew nothing but the fact of itself, for there was nothing else for it to know. But it could feel, and what it felt was meaninglessness of a kind never known by anything since, because there was no other thing that could perceive the All Life and so give it meaning.

"Then the All Life began to grow. By the very act of growing, it created another place, a place where there was space and time, and so the All Life created space and time as well. At first, this other place, where there was space and time, and which would one day be called the world, was without light, without heat and without life. And yet, into this dark and dead place, some forms of the All Life began to appear. The first form was what would one day be called fire, common to all living things, but which now formed first the sun and then the moon. The next form was what would one day be called air, until the world, that was yet to become the world, was filled with it. The light from the fire of the sun and the moon began to warm the air, until what would one day be called water began to fall, the first rain that ever was. And after the longest time, although there were still none to call it time, further forms of the All Life began to appear in the world as earth, then grass, trees and all other things that live in the ground. And then finally, when the All Life had almost filled the world with itself in these forms, it began to appear as animals and at last as people. And by so doing, it fulfilled what had always been its true, although unknown purpose, to become alive. Because a thing not perceived to be alive cannot truly live at all."

The Skull-Faced Woman draws a deep breath, then screams at the top of her voice.

"We are the All Life, and the All Life is Us."

She pauses as though awaiting a response. Suddenly I know what I am meant to say, and I say it. As I do, my voice is the voice of hundreds.

"We are the All Life, and the All Life is Us."

The Skull-Faced Woman pauses again, stands back and looks down at the huge rock on which she is standing that is now both the House of Women and House of Men. Then several of the adults with torches step closer to it, holding the flames close to the carvings on it so that once again they seem to move.

"We are the All Life," repeats the Skull-Faced Woman. "Forget this, and we will become like the Lost Ones, so called because they turned from all others and so turned from life to endless death. But if you remain children, you will forget. So you can be children no longer."

Again, her words appear to be some kind of signal, this time to the men and women herding the girls and boys, because now they start to push their charges forward. This makes the lines break a little here and there, but even so, both lines move quickly. For several moments nothing happens. Then the Skull-Faced Woman puts her head back and screams again.

Her scream goes on for several moments, and although it sounds more animal than human, it seems to have a curiously excited quality to it. When it stops, for a few moments, everyone, including the Skull-Faced Woman herself, is still. Then a large, dark shape emerges from the long skirts covering the Skull-Faced Woman's widely planted legs. Slowly and very uncertainly, the shape unfolds, revealing itself to be a boy, perhaps twelve or thirteen years old. He is covered from head to foot in what looks like blood and is attached to the Skull-Faced Woman by a thick cord tied around his waist, the other end of which leads up underneath the skirts of the Skull-Faced Woman.

The boy stands for a moment, shaking, dazed and plainly terrified. In total silence, the Skull-Faced Woman raises her right hand, in which she seems to be holding something. From this distance I cannot see what it is, but it seems to be some kind of knife because she uses it to cut the cord connecting her to the boy. As the severed cord drops, the Skull-Faced Woman suddenly lunges at the boy and pushes him violently. His arms flailing, the boy slithers backwards and falls off the steep rock and into the upraised arms of the people below, who are now yelling and hooting in wild elation.

For what seems like hours, one bloody figure after another appears from beneath the skirts of the Skull-Faced Woman. Each one is tethered to her in the same way as the first, cut loose with the same implement and then thrust off the rock and into the crowd of men and women who catch them, set them upright, then pass them rapidly backwards, constantly patting, stroking, hugging and even kissing them.

Finally, the last one has gone. I watch the Skull-Faced Woman, still standing in her triumphant pose, but when I look around again, the three huge fires and all the people, except for the Skull-Faced Woman, have vanished.

"What will happen to all the people that were here?" I ask the voice.

Before it can answer, I hear a sound, and I turn around to see the Skull-Faced Woman standing facing me. Even though she is now so much closer to me, she actually looks rather less terrifying, partly because of the human eyes I can now see watching me through the gaping sockets of her skull mask, but also because of her mouth, at which I find myself staring: I have never seen anyone over the age of ten with all their own teeth.

"We have had to do this so many times," the Skull-Faced Woman says.

"We?" I repeat.

"There have been so many dangers," she goes on, as if I haven't spoken. "So many times when it looked as though we could never survive. Each time we have to decide how we will meet the new threat. How we must change in order to do so. Now, the danger is the Great Cold."

"It is killing us all," I reply.

"No," says the Skull-Faced Woman. "It will kill very many of us, to be sure. But not all. Some will survive. But survival is only possible through constant change. Change by doing new things, or change by doing old things in new ways. Those who are changing from children to adults always learn this lesson best. That is why we do this. Yet something else will soon threaten us, then something else again. One day, we must learn how to break this circle, learn not just how to meet the dangers as they arise, but how to stop them from arising at all. But we must take great care that in doing so, we do not become like the Lost Ones."

She turns, gesturing at the carvings on the face of the huge rock outcrop behind her.

"Yet we did learn long ago that there is one thing above all that we must do, if are not to become like them. We learnt never to forget that each and every person must live not merely for themselves, but for everyone, not just in their own time but in all times."

Although her skull mask prevents me seeing her eyes properly, I still feel her gaze on me.

"Wouldn't you say?" she asks me.

I do not reply, too startled by both the sudden change in her tone from the portentous to the casually chatty and by the question itself. But it seems that the Skull-Faced Woman does not expect any answer. Instead, she stoops slightly as she reaches round behind her back, then straightens again, holding out what she has taken from her belt. I realise straight away that it must be the implement she used to cut the cords connecting her to each of the boys and girls appearing from beneath her skirts in the ceremony I have just watched.

She holds the thing out to me. It is indeed some kind of knife, with two parallel rows of ten or so small flint blades fixed with pine resin into slots notched in the wood. However, the dark brown wood holding them, instead of being more or less straight like a normal knife, has been carved almost into the shape of a crescent moon. As I stare at it, the Skull-Faced Woman again proffers it towards me, hilt first.

"Go on," she says. "It's all right. You can hold it if you like."

Carefully, I take the strange, curved knife from her. As well as being this peculiar shape, it is heavy and strangely balanced. I stare down at it, turning it over in my hands. It looks utterly unlike anything else I have ever seen, and yet the heft and weight of it are familiar, and I feel that although I cannot recall it just now, this thing has a name almost as familiar to me as my own. I look up at the Skull-Faced Woman.

"This is old," I say. "Really old."

She does not reply. I look down again at the knife.

"It's nothing like a normal knife. Why is it this strange shape?"

"It was made to be fit for its purpose, I suppose," the Skull-Faced Woman replies, her tone still light. "Like any good tool. You have seen the purpose for which I have used it. It may have others. Perhaps you can show me one."

I am too surprised by her words to do anything more than stare at her.

"It's all right," the Skull-Faced Woman says. "You can take off your mittens."

It does not occur to me to argue with her. I place the strange, curved knife carefully on the surface of the snow around my feet and remove my mittens, which I leave dangling from the sinew strings securing them to my hooded cloak. Then I pick the curved knife up again. I look around helplessly.

"I should try to find some food," I say.

The Skull-Faced Woman shrugs. "I dare say you should," she replies casually.

"But there are no tracks to show me where to look," I add, feeling the need to explain.

She shrugs again.

"Why not just look anyway? You never know. Look, and you might find."

Again, it does not occur to me to disobey. Very slowly and carefully, so that I don't damage my boots or, as importantly, so that I don't begin sweating, I start to kick down and around in the powdery snow in which I am standing until I have cleared a small area. Then I squat down and, in an action that suddenly feels as natural as breathing or walking, I begin to swing the curved knife downwards into the surface of the older, compacted snow. The combination of the knife's weight and shape means that its pointed tip easily breaks up the hard snow, loosening it enough for me to start digging down with my hands until I reach the frozen soil beneath. I am worried that my fingers will become totally numb before I can find anything, but then suddenly I see a spot of bright green. I pick up the curved knife again, and carefully using its pointed tip, I expose a broad green leaf with dark red flecks. I look up at the Skull-Faced Woman, who has been watching me silently all this time.

"I told you," she says quietly. "What have you found?"

For a few moments, I don't know what to say, as she must know what the plant is just as well as I do. Yet this time, it seems that she does expect an answer.

"It's sorrel," I reply.

Suddenly, I see another bright green spot peeping out from under the lumps of broken compacted snow. Then another, then a third. Delicately, I use the point of the curved knife to uncover not just one stem but what is clearly part of a large bed.

"Lots of sorrel," I add.

"You seem very pleased," the Skull-Faced Woman remarks.

"Of course I am," I reply. "There's enough here for everyone in my entire clan."

The Skull-Faced Woman simply looks at me. "Enough for what?"

Yet again I am at a loss for an answer, not understanding why she does not understand.

"It's sorrel," I say again. "If we can get sorrel to eat, we won't get nearly so many pains in our hips and knees. And our hair and teeth won't fall out, not like they do now."

I look down again at the precious green and red plant and eagerly begin tugging at one of the root stems.

"Stop."

The command in the Skull-Faced Woman's voice is unmistakeable, and I immediately stop pulling at the sorrel. I look up at her.

"Better to cut it, wouldn't you say?" she asks, her voice reverting to its earlier mild conversational tone. "If you pull it all up, there won't be enough for more than a few meals, will there?"

She seems to incline her head slightly to my right, where I have placed the curved knife. I pick it up again and, using the flint blades along its edge, begin to cut as much sorrel as I can without hurting the root system, so that it will carry on growing. When I have placed the cuttings in the deerskin pouch hanging from my belt, I look up at the Skull-Faced Woman again.

"Thank you," I say.

In the silence that follows, I find from somewhere the courage to ask the question I have wanted to ask since I first saw her.

"Who are you?"

In answer, the Skull-Faced Woman reaches up and unties the leather thongs holding her bone mask in position. Finally understanding, I put the curved knife in my left hand, and with my right I reach up to take the mask from her and find myself looking at Arlen.

"Oh," I say. "I don't mean to be rude or anything, but do I know you? I do, don't I?"

Arlen smiles.

"In a way," she says. "But the real question is, do you know who you are?"

"Yes," I reply. "Of course I do."

I don't know why I say this, because when I wake up, I realise it isn't true.

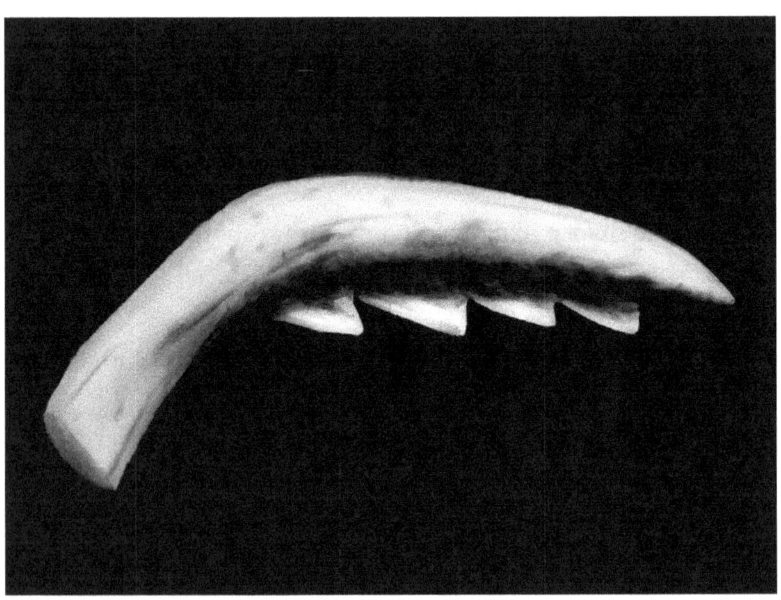

After four days' walking, we are once again amongst the villages of the Northern Federation: our old home. No one wants to visit the old site of our village, but we are made very welcome at the other villages, amongst whom many of our party still have relatives. But then, after only another three days, we reach the end of the trees and the beginning of the Sea of Grass.

Naturally, I have told Arlen straight away of what I have seen the night before we set off, but neither of us is able to explain what it means, nor why I have seen it when she hasn't. But we cannot talk about it at any length for fear of being overheard by one of the others, and we are in any case busy enough looking for food from known locations along the trail—we have brought some with us, but it will not be enough—and, in particular, protecting our Fire that Arlen is carrying.

The Fire is in the form of a burning block of fungus held in the Fire-Box, a small container made of sections of lightweight beaver bone, glued with birch tar reinforced with hazel dowels and held onto Arlen's belt by a fine but very tough nettle-twine net. The box has several small holes drilled through it to ensure a steady flow of air, and with this, our Fire will continue to burn without any other attendance really being required. Arlen's first task is therefore to make sure that this air supply is not interrupted as she carries the Fire. Torban has already shown her how to walk in order to achieve this, and although for the first day she finds this quite difficult, she soon comes to rely on the rest of us to help her make sure that she stays on the trail and doesn't fall into a puddle or a stream.

We continue to trudge through the mist. Rona is staring intently at the ground and what seems like every single tree, although she stops quite frequently to peer up through the forest canopy at the pale and barely visible sun, lips moving as she tries to persuade him to dispel the mist faster.

It's rather dull going, but on the second day after leaving the last village, Arlen and I are joined by Karel. It very quickly becomes apparent that he wants to talk to Arlen but has no idea how actually to begin a conversation with her. So more to break the awkward silence than anything else, Arlen asks Karel what he knows about wheat.

He is silent for several moments before answering.

"Ah yes, wheat," he says finally, as though about to confess something deeply embarrassing. "Well, I know where it grows, obviously. And how to get there. I know a bit about how to gather it, and I even know a bit about how to make bread out of it. But apart from that, I'm afraid I don't really know any more about it than anyone else."

We trudge on in silence for a few moments. But then I see that Karel is absent-mindedly fiddling with something hanging from the back of his belt, and I realise that he started doing so the moment Arlen spoke to him. The thing is moving, swinging gently against the back of his thigh with every step, so it takes me a few moments more to recognize it. When I do, I stop, staring. Arlen notices, and muttering an apology to Karel, she hurries over to me.

"What is it?" she whispers. "What's the matter?"

"Ask him about that thing hanging from his belt," I just about manage to whisper, pointing.

Arlen looks at me quizzically, but I shake my head and point more urgently. So, with a look of frustration mingled with helplessness, Arlen turns back and catches Karel up.

"What's that thing you've got on your belt there?" she asks him innocently.

Karel frowns at her in what to me looks like dismay. Then he stops walking and with a sigh, takes off the bow that has been slung across his chest, half-turns, and unties the thongs holding the strange object to his belt. He straightens and holds the object out to Arlen. I have been half-wondering if I could have been mistaken, but I can see now that I have not. It is a knife, but unlike any other I have ever seen, except once: the dark wood into which the blades have been set has been carved almost into the shape of a crescent moon.

As Arlen stares at the strange thing, Karel rather awkwardly proffers it towards her, hilt first.

"Go on," he says. "It's all right. You can hold it if you like."

Arlen glances at me, and although I am still too surprised to speak, I step over to her side, nodding at her. She looks back at Karel and gingerly takes the strange, curved knife from him, turning slowly over and over as she examines it. Then, clearly finding it a lot heavier than expected, she hefts it gently. The expression on her face is one of intrigue yet puzzlement. Then her mouth falls open, and I know she has finally recognized it.

"It's like you described it," she says to me in a barely audible whisper. "Just like it."

"Yes," I whisper back. "Except that it's not just like it. It is it. It's the same knife."

"This is old," says Arlen, studying the knife. "Really, really old."

"Sorry?" says Karel, assuming that Arlen is speaking to him. She frowns and clears her throat.

"I said, it's really old." Arlen holds the blade closer to her face. "It's nothing like a normal knife. Why has it been made in this strange shape?" She looks up at Karel. "What's it actually for?"

Karel now has large red patches on each cheek, and he is gnawing his lip so hard I'm slightly concerned that he's going to make it bleed. I have recovered a little from the shock of recognizing the curved knife and I look at him closely, trying to work out why Arlen's questions are making him so very uncomfortable.

"To be honest," he replies after a long pause, "no one really knows. Someone traded it to my Great-Great-Grandda ages ago. It was clearly really old then, but the man who traded it didn't know what it was. Anyway, it's been passed from generation to generation ever since. My Ma says—said—"

He stops suddenly. His mother Fara, a nice woman, went with the White Plague three years earlier. Karel swallows.

"She told me what her Da told her. That my Great-Great-Grandda always said that he wanted it just because it's such a beautiful thing. But you can tell that it was used a lot. Look."

Taking the strange, curved knife back from Arlen, he lifts it up close to her face and points to where several of the small flint blades are chipped and worn down through prolonged use. I am still staring at him rather than at the curved knife, and as I do so, I begin to get an odd feeling that Arlen is on the point of seeing something that is very important, and that it is just as important that somebody other than her and me should see it. Then, as I am wondering what this thing might be, I see Karel and Arlen bent over the strange knife so that their heads touch, and they both look up. They stare into one another's eyes for a few moments. Then Arlen frowns slightly and draws her head back, and the instant she does so, Karel does the same. He clears his throat and looks back at the knife, scrutinizing it with renewed intensity.

"But it looks to me like it was made for both cutting and digging," he says, speaking a little too rapidly. "Look."

Suddenly he drops to his knees, grabs a clump of grass in one hand and with only a couple of sideways hacks at the clump's base with the knife cuts it clean through. He puts the handful of grass on one side and then, swinging the knife downwards in a, delicate chopping action, digs out the root system of the clump of grass he has just cut. He stands up again, holding out the cut grass and its roots to Arlen.

"See?"

Arlen frowns at the cut grass, then at Karel.

"Well, yes. But why would anyone go to all the trouble of making something like this just to cut grass? Or dig up its roots?"

Karel shrugs. Then suddenly, I understand. "Not just any grass," I whisper to Arlen. "Wheat."

Arlen looks at me and then at Karel. "Is that it?" she asks him, forgetting for a moment that he hasn't heard me. "Was this made for wheat? To cut it? And to gather its roots?"

Karel shrugs unhappily.

"I don't know," he says.

Arlen frowns again.

"But why are you so—"

She stops as I put my hand on her arm and whisper to her again. "He believes it was made by the Lost Ones."

Arlen looks at me, shocked, but I shake my head. "It's all

right, it wasn't. It's very old, but it isn't from their time. And anyway, the Lost Ones didn't use things like this. Most of them didn't know how to."

Arlen continues to stare at me. I shrug.

She turns from me to the miserable-looking Karel, but before she can say anything to him, I put my hand back on her arm and whisper to her. "Perhaps he doesn't need to know that just yet."

*

None of this has taken very long and soon the three of us have caught up with the rest of our party. We have been walking only for another hour before Rona glances upwards, stops, and holds up her hand.

"We'll camp here tonight."

There is still a good two hours of daylight left, but if we keep walking, we will reach the edge of the trees and the beginning of the Sea of Grass just as night is falling, which would be most unwise. So we make camp and build a fire, Arlen again transferring our Fire to it so that anyone who wants to speak to their families can do so.

We get up at dawn the next day, and after we have breakfasted, Rona tells us to put on the otter-pelt jackets that we have so far been carrying in our rucksacks: over the last three days, the temperature has been falling steadily. We resume walking and soon we arrive at the very edge of the trees and the only world most of us have ever known.

It still strikes me as odd that such a huge change can come about so quickly. One moment I am only vaguely aware that the trees are becoming more and more sparse, and the next, I and the others are all standing by a lonely-looking birch beyond which there is nothing but grass and open blue sky. We all stop.

"Well, here we are," says Rona, rather unnecessarily.

She turns around to face the rest of us.

"Last chance."

117

We all know what she is asking us, but no one says anything. Without another word, Rona turns again and, with only the faintest hesitation, puts up her hood and steps out under the open sky.

I look at Arlen. She too has put her hood up and her head is bent down against the cold wind. She seems steady enough on her feet, but she has gone very quiet. I lean over to her and whisper.

"Are you sure you're all right?"

She nods without raising her eyes. Suddenly there is a loud retching sound, and we both turn to see Finn on his knees, bent over and being sick onto the ground. Before anyone else can react, Rona turns quickly and strides over to him. She squats down next to him with one arm laid gently across his back until he stops vomiting, then helps him wipe his face with a few handfuls of grass. He is still shuddering, but Rona then puts both her arms around him and holds him tightly for several long moments, gently rocking him. After doing this for a few moments, she says something else to him—the rest of us are too far away to hear what—and he nods hesitantly. Then Rona hauls him back to his feet and pulls his head down to hers until their foreheads are touching. She speaks to him again, smoothing his hair with her hand all the while, although again, her voice is too low for anyone else to hear what she is saying. Then Finn nods once more as though in answer, and this time his nod is more decisive.

Gently, Rona releases him, considers him for a moment, then turns again and walks briskly back to where the rest of us are waiting.

"It's all right," she says, smiling cheerfully. "He's fine."

*

We walk for four hours or so directly into the cold wind over what looks to me like totally featureless grassland, my eyes fixed on the ground just ahead of me. When finally I feel I can risk a glance upwards, I see rather to my surprise that Karel and not Rona is leading the way. But then I notice that Rona is both watching him and occasionally checking the way ahead herself, and I realise that Karel is learning how to navigate a wheat gathering party over the Sea of Grass. He is clearly doing pretty well because after only another five hours' continuous walking and just a couple more minor mishaps—Madoc briefly breaking down, then Finn again, Rona attending to them in the same way each time, before the rest of us can put Torban's instructions into practice—Karel stops. He turns to Rona, pointing proudly to something on the horizon. She nods and gives him a congratulatory pat on the shoulder. He grins at her delightedly, suddenly looking about eleven years old. Seeing this, Arlen can't help laughing. Karel hears her, and for a moment, he looks rather vexed. Then he smiles a little, rueful smile at her.

Of course the rest of us have absolutely no idea where we are, so we simply cluster around Rona and Karel. Huddling together against the wind and carefully avoiding glancing up into the gaping sky, we all look to where Rona is pointing. After allowing a few moments for my eyes to adjust, I make out several stick-like shapes about five hundred paces away. It takes a few moments more to realise that they're not moving.

"What are they? Are they people?" demands Gorn, voice hoarse with apprehension, all his usual cockiness suddenly absent.

Karel looks at Rona, who nods her permission to him.

"No," Karel replies, voice raised over the wind. "Not people. One of the old wheat gathering camps. It's what we've been aiming for."

We resume walking and soon we arrive at what looks like a miniature version of our village but with all the houses, or rather huts, partially dismantled, consisting only of their hazel-wand frames. In the centre, I can see where there was once a fire. Then I look up to see Karel again pointing, this time at a large patch of grass about thirty paces beyond the remains of the outermost hut frame. I look at it, then back at Karel.

"Is that it?" Suma asks him.

Karel nods. "That's it. That's the wheat."

It looks very similar to other grasses, except that it's rather taller, most of it growing to about my height, and having larger ears. Even so, there is some excitement at seeing what we have come so far to collect, and Arlen, Suma, Madoc, Finn and I start towards it. But we then hear Rona's loud and suddenly commanding voice.

"Stop."

We all stop and remain motionless as Rona strides past us and up to the edge of the patch where she halts, peering up intently at the ears as they wave about, first one, then several others. Then she drops to the ground and appears to study something lying there. After a few moments, she stands up and peers closely at the wheat once more. Everyone else looks as puzzled by this as I feel, except for Karel. Arlen steps silently over to him and stands on tiptoe, tugging his hood aside to whisper into his ear.

"What's she doing?"

He turns his head towards Arlen, although he doesn't take his eyes from Rona.

"She's looking to see how many of the seed pods haven't fallen or burst," he whispers back. "She's got to be very careful because some of them are really delicate. One brush and—"

He holds up his hand in a fist to mimic a seed pod, then suddenly opens it, fingers splayed.

"It's all gone."

After a few moments, Rona steps back from the wheat patch and walks back, nodding in apparent satisfaction.

"Not bad," she says to Karel quietly. "Not bad at all. It looks like we could be in luck."

Karel is clearly hugely flattered at Rona speaking to him almost as though he were as experienced as she is. Trying hard not to show it, he simply nods knowingly.

Rona turns around to face the rest of us.

"We'll start gathering tomorrow. There are quite a few patches like this nearby, so we'll make camp here. We can use those," she goes on, nodding towards the bare tent frames. "They should be perfectly serviceable."

Relieved at not having to re-erect our own tent frames, we start unpacking the hides, although as Suma and Madoc are pulling one of them over one of the old frames, it collapses. They look rather reproachfully at Rona. She just laughs.

"Oh dear. Not that serviceable after all, then."

*

The next day, Rona takes us to seven other clumps of wheat nearby, each one of roughly similar size to the first, about forty paces long and rather less wide. After carefully inspecting each one, Rona pronounces herself satisfied, although it is past noon by the time we have returned to the first patch of wheat, where Rona starts showing us how to gather it.

"As you'll have realised by now," she says, as she reaches up to start carefully plucking ears from the stalks, "this can be quite tricky. Come in a bit closer so you can see. Be careful though."

We all gather round to get a good look at exactly what Rona is doing, although, as instructed, we take care not to touch the wheat.

"Wheat's just like most other grasses," Rona continues. "When it ripens, the seed pods on these ears split open, especially when they're blown about by the wind. But although we know roughly when the wheat ripens, we don't know exactly when the seeds pods will split. And that's always been the problem with the wheat that grows near where we live, amongst the trees."

She takes a step back, still scrutinizing the wheat as it waves slowly in the cold, constant wind. Then she looks back over her shoulder.

"So why, you're probably wondering, do we have to come all the way out here?"

"Because some of this wheat's different," replies Arlen immediately.

Rona looks at her for several moments. It is obvious from the expression on her face that she hasn't expected anyone to answer her.

"That's right," she says at last, nodding. "Some of this wheat's different."

She looks at Arlen for a few moments more, then turns back to the wheat. When she speaks again, she does so in her usual bright and brisk tone.

"It's different in two ways. First, as you can see, there's a lot more of it here, which means we have a better chance of finding more ripe seed pods that haven't split yet. But more importantly, some of these seed pods don't open even when they're ripe. If they're not picked, they'll just wither, without the seed inside ever dispersing. Something to do with the wind here, maybe. Or the bright sunshine. But no one really knows."

Rona puts the seed pods she has picked into the old hide bag slung around her shoulders.

"You can't really tell which is which until you've tried to pick some of them," she goes on. "So that means you have to be really careful in case you've got one that does split, because if you have, it's really easy to crush it under your fingers. Now then, let's see."

She reaches out and plucks a few of the seed pods from a ripe stalk. They come free easily enough, as do the ones on the next one she chooses, then the next, although some come apart as she picks them. But the next one she selects clearly gives her significantly more difficulty. Finally, she snaps the whole ear off the stalk and steps back again, holding it up for our inspection.

"Well, there you are," she says. "Like I said just now, and well, as you've just seen, you don't know which kind is which until you've tried to pick it."

She places the ear in the goatskin bag at her waist then looks around at us.

"That's pretty much all there is to it. Be careful, be delicate, and obviously, try and get as much as you can."

Rona then takes each member of the party to a different part of the wheat patch and shows them where they are to pick. I stand close to Arlen, but she has only been picking the wheat for about an hour or so when she moves her bag around to her back so that it's out of her way, and starts examining individual ears closely.

"What is it?" I ask her quietly. She frowns.

"These seed pods. The ones that Rona said are different. Look."

I look closely at them. Then Arlen reaches out to pluck an ear from its stalk. She has to twist it before it comes free and when it does, it's still completely intact. She holds it up to me. I shrug.

"It's like she said just now. For some reason, this sort of seed pod doesn't open, even when it's ripe."

Arlen plucks another ear and rolls it gently between her fingers. I can see that just as it takes her a little effort to detach the seed pods from the ear, it also takes an effort to crush them and release the seed. She looks up.

"There are quite a few like that," she says. "Almost as though they were waiting to be picked."

"Did you say something?" asks Rona, who has walked back over to us. Arlen glances at her and smiles, quite unperturbed.

"Yes," she says. "I said there are quite a few of the ones that don't split. Almost as though they're just waiting to be picked."

Rona nods. Then she sees the look on Arlen's face. "What is it?"

Arlen shakes her head. "I don't know. It might be nothing."

Rona looks at her in silence for several moments. Then she grunts. "Then again, it might be something."

Arlen nods. "Yes," she says. "Yes, it might."

*

Arlen and I spend the next three days examining the wheat to get an idea of how much of it is made up of this odd sort, where the seed pods don't drop or open. Then on the third day, something else occurs to Arlen.

"What is it now?" I ask her, suddenly noticing that she is still just staring at the wheat.

She doesn't reply but turns and waves a beckoning arm at

123

Karel. After a few moments, he sees her, says something to Rona and walks over, looking at Arlen quizzically.

"That funny old curved knife of yours," Arlen says to him. "The one that looks like it was made to cut grass and dig up its roots."

Karel frowns. "What about it?" He sounds slightly defensive.

"Well," Arlen continues, "wheat's a type of grass, isn't it? But we're not cutting it, are we? Or digging up its roots. We're picking it."

Karel frowns again. Then he shakes his head. "I'm sorry, but I don't see what you're getting at. If we cut the wheat here, we'd have to carry everything we've cut, including all the stalks, all the way home, when all we want are the seed pods."

Luckily, he doesn't see the look of mild exasperation that Arlen gives me.

"No, I understand that," she says. "But surely that must have been true for whoever made your strange knife."

Karel looks at her blankly.

"So, if it was," Arlen goes on patiently, "what was the point of making it?"

Karel shrugs. "I don't know. Maybe they just happened to have some big wheat patches like this right next to wherever they lived."

"Maybe," replies Arlen. "Or maybe they used your curved knife to put it there."

Karel stares at her. "What do you mean, put it there?" he asks after a few moments.

Arlen shakes her head. "Never mind." She looks at Karel. "It will all become clear to you later. I promise it will."

That night, Arlen gets Karel to show Rona his curved knife, and all three talk for a long time, although without arriving at any conclusion. Over the next few days, Arlen and I carry on examining patches of wheat. All of them include a substantial proportion of the kind whose ripe seed pods do not drop but clearly will just wither on the stalk without opening unless they are picked. None of the rest of our party seems to mind the fact that we are not gathering wheat at anything like the same speed as them, except of course for Gorn, who makes several snide and increasingly unpleasant remarks about Arlen. It isn't until Karel threatens to hit him that I finally understand the real reason for Gorn's bitterness towards her. I am silently reproaching myself for my stupidity when I look up and see Breccan watching me.

"What are you doing here?" I hiss at him. "Where's Rod? Why aren't you both with Ma?"

Then I see the look on his face. "What's the matter?"

"Rod's with Ma and Da," says Breccan quickly. "It's one of the reasons I've come here. To tell you."

He takes a deep breath. "It's the baby. Ma's new baby. He's arrived too early. And he's—"

He drops his eyes, biting his lip.

"Oh no," I whisper.

Breccan just nods miserably, and we stand in silence.

"What's the other reason?" I ask after a few moments.

"What?" he asks, looking blank. Then he collects himself. "Oh yes. The other reason. Arlen."

It's my turn to frown.

"What about her?"

Breccan sighs heavily.

"We need to talk to her. To warn her again. About Gorn."

*

So Breccan and I try to warn Arlen about Gorn, although we decide that we won't tell her yet about our new baby brother. But as neither of us can be very specific about what we are warning Arlen against, we don't get very far.

"I know he's thoroughly unpleasant and that he seems to have some particular problem with me," Arlen finally says, in a slightly exasperated tone of voice. "But I don't know what you expect me to do about it."

Breccan frowns and turns to me for help.

"Well," I say carefully, "I suppose what we're saying is, just be careful around him."

Arlen sighs and gives me a long look. Suddenly, she smiles. Still smiling, she stoops again to finish strapping the tent hide to its carrying frame with nettle twine rope, carries it over to Madoc and lifts it onto his back. When she is satisfied that he has adjusted it properly, she walks back over to the two of us.

"Look, I know you're just trying to look after me. And I'm grateful. No, really. I am. And I promise that I will be careful. All right?"

Both Breccan and I, and Karel, although neither of us has spoken to him about it, watch Gorn very carefully the whole time on our journey back. But he doesn't do or say anything. In fact, he seems unusually quiet, not even making his usual sarcastic remarks about anyone, and completely ignoring Arlen.

As soon as we return to the village, Rona makes her report to the Elders. She asks Arlen to accompany her, and as usual, I go with Arlen. The meeting takes place in Serris' house, and although everyone listens very politely, neither Arlen nor Rona can explain why the seed pods that don't split might be especially important, and the meeting ends rather unsatisfactorily.

I feel that I need to help Arlen more with this, but just now I have to see my mother. As Breccan has warned me, our new baby brother, Little Bran, has arrived far too early and is therefore far too small. He can't breathe properly and although my mother is producing a respectable amount of milk, rather surprisingly given how hungry everyone is all the time, Little Bran can keep hardly any down, so he isn't growing as he should. Sometimes, early babies survive—Edra was early, and she was a very strong baby and is by this time an even stronger toddler—but it is already clear that our new baby brother won't be one of them.

Unusually, therefore, my mother needs me to be near to her. I very quickly grow used to the funny sound of Little Bran's breathing and the look in his eyes as he constantly gazes around, as though trying to see as much of this world as he can in the few days he will have in it. Arlen of course understands that I cannot spend as much time with her, but one cold morning I check to see that Little Bran is still asleep, tucked up next to our sleeping mother, and decide to go over to the goat pen.

Gently taking hold of the dung-encrusted fur around a goat's anus and then cutting it away with a small blade so that maggots don't breed inside the goat isn't exactly enjoyable, but it has to be done, and in fact Arlen and I have never minded doing it. It's such a smelly job that we tend to be left to ourselves, which is nice. There is always the risk of being kicked if the blade cuts the goat, or sometimes even when it doesn't, particularly by one of the new billies that we have to acquire each year to improve the bloodline. But even so, it's very peaceful just squatting there chatting as Arlen gently saws away at the filthy fur. Neither of us has exactly forgotten Breccan's warning about Gorn, but it's so pleasant just being on our own in the cold quiet of the early morning that any kind of danger seems a long way away. Until that is, I glance up and see Gorn watching Arlen with a very odd look on his face.

"I knew I'd find you here," he says. "Here, along with all the other goats' arses."

It's clear from his contrived snigger that he hasn't come here just to insult us. Arlen sighs and looks up at him. "What do you want?"

Gorn ignores her question, but after a few moments he speaks again.

"I hear your friend's new little brother won't last. When he goes, that'll make four, won't it?"

Arlen turns in disgust and carries on with her cutting.

"What's the matter with you?" Gorn suddenly spits out. He gestures furiously at the goats, who start away from him nervously. "Who would want to sit for hours on end with the goats? Picking around in their shitty backsides?"

Arlen looks up again to stare at Gorn for several long moments before replying.

"Oh, it's not that bad, "she says at last. "Compared to who I could be with. Or who and what I could be looking at."

She looks pointedly at Gorn's crippled foot. Then her lips tighten as though she is trying not to laugh, and she turns back again to the goat. "But yes," she goes on in a carefree tone, resuming her cutting. "It is a shame about Maya's new little brother. It's a shame about Breccan, Rod and Maya too, come to that."

She pauses. When she carries on speaking, it's as though she's speaking more to herself than to Gorn.

"Surprising too, really. After all, look at their father. Such a strong man, Bran is. Big, but agile with it. Graceful, almost. I suppose that's what makes him such a good hunter. He's powerful, but he moves so well. So light on his feet."

She sits back, looks again at the now furious red-faced Gorn, then again and very pointedly down at his crippled foot. "I mean, he doesn't need a stick to get about, does he?"

Gorn is silent for a long time. Then he swallows, leans down to Arlen and lowers his voice to a hiss.

"You may have fooled everyone else, you little bitch, but you haven't fooled me. I know what you're doing. You want to be like the Traveller. But I know you're a fraud, and I'm going to prove it. Your mother won't be around to protect you forever, and when she's gone, I'll show everyone just what a fraud you are. And when I do, they'll take you to the Law Sayers, and they'll say that we should do something very, very bad to you. And it just so happens that I have a few ideas about that."

He grips Arlen's shoulder, and suddenly she and I know exactly what Gorn wants to do to her and how badly he means to hurt her. Arlen jumps up and twists away from him. I slap him around his face several times with both hands, which of course has no effect on him at all. But when he lunges at Arlen again, she thrusts her hand into his clothes around his groin and grabs something. Then she pulls hard on what she has grabbed, twisting it violently at the same time. Gorn screams and doubles up while at the same time trying to drag Arlen's hand away, but that only makes her pull and twist harder. So Gorn tries to punch her instead, but he can't do that either because she has pressed her head into his chest to stop him getting a proper swing. For a few moments they are locked in this ridiculous position, the only sounds being their panting and the frightened goats skittering about, and my head is full of Gorn's desire to hurt Arlen, to hurt her more than he has ever wanted to hurt anyone else. Then Gorn manages to wrench himself free from Arlen's grip, and I see the small knife he now has in his right hand. For several seconds, all three of us are motionless. I'm aware that someone else nearby is shouting, but I don't have time to look to see who it is because Gorn has suddenly lunged at Arlen again, the knife in his hand stabbing down towards her bare neck. He's very quick, but before his blow can land I have somehow managed to step between them.

But then Arlen, Gorn, the goats and the village all disappear.

*

Again, I feel a strange sensation of being pulled through a long passageway. I know I should be worried about Gorn continuing to attack Arlen with his knife, but stupidly I find myself wondering whose house this passageway can be part of and why I have never seen it before. But before I can become too puzzled by this, I see that I am heading towards the light at its end, so I am not going inside but outside, which doesn't make any sense because surely I am already outside with Arlen and the goats. But again there is no time to be too puzzled because now I am outside, standing on an open space that's like the Sea of Grass in that there's nothing to see except grass and sky, yet unlike it in that there is no cold wind, merely a pleasantly warm breeze. And the intense feeling of belonging, of being truly alive, is even stronger than when I met the voice in the air all those years before.

I find that for some reason, I can't look upwards quite in the same way I can back in my world, but I can see enough of the sky to know it's a fine day, and although I can feel the sun on my back, it isn't hot, just pleasantly warm. I can feel the breeze on my flanks, and I can hear it gently rustling the grass. But I can't see or hear anything else at all: no birds, no goats, not even any insects. Then, just as I am starting to wonder if I am going to hear the voice, I do.

"You're all right, Maya," it says quietly but very firmly. "And so is Arlen. She is safe. Gorn will not harm her."

This is some relief, but I am by no means entirely convinced.

"But he's got that knife," I say, vaguely aware that like before, I can hear what I am saying without speaking, but just now too worried to care. "He stabbed me. He meant to stab Arlen. I got in the way, and he stabbed me instead. And he means to hurt Arlen. I mean really hurt her."

"Yes, I know he does," replies the voice sadly. "Gorn is a very troubled and very dangerous young man. But in fact, he didn't stab Arlen. And he won't be able to try to hurt her, or anyone else, ever again. She has already seen to that."

"Who has?" I ask, surprised.

There's a long pause.

"Serris."

"You know Serris?"

"Oh yes," says the voice quickly. "Actually, I know her a lot better than she has ever realised."

I am confused. Not just by what the voice has said, but by the unmistakeable note of bitterness in the way she has said it.

"But how can you be so sure?" I ask finally. "That Gorn won't hurt Arlen, I mean?"

When finally the voice speaks again, it is sadder than I have ever heard it.

"You won't be here with me for long, Maya. And by the time you return, you will understand how I can be so certain."

I know I have no choice but to accept this. And in any case, two new questions have just occurred to me.

"But then why am I here? And where is here?"

"There's someone else to see you," says the voice softly. "Perhaps that might give you a better idea."

I hear a soft scuffling sound behind me.

Turning, I see a small, very young brown and black foal

about ten paces away, just standing there watching me. I look back at the brown and black foal, and suddenly I know who he is.

Little Bran trots forward and I stretch out my neck as he stretches his up until our noses are touching. He stands still and lets me rub my nose gently against his, then against his stubbly little mane. For a few moments, I enjoy the smell of him. Then he turns and trots away, and when I look up—at least, as far as I can look up—I see a vast herd of horses. I have never seen horses before, but somehow I know that this herd is hundreds of times bigger than any back in my world. The individual horses I can make out before they all merge into one huge dark mass are just standing quietly, some cropping the grass, others sniffing the warm air. As Little Bran joins them, two mares give him a welcoming nuzzle, and as I watch them, the familiar feeling of intense belonging washes over me once more.

"Do you know where we are now?" asks the voice.

"Yes," I say. "It's where we were before, even though it looks so different. It's the All Life, isn't it? And so are you, aren't you? You're the All Life."

There's another pause, and this time I sense awkwardness.

"Actually, that's rather hard to say."

I have been so certain that my guess was right, that this answer, together with the shock of Gorn's attack, of suddenly arriving here, wherever here is, and then of seeing my little brother, makes me lose my temper completely. All at once, I am raving.

"What do you mean, that's rather hard to say? How dare you not know? What's the point of you if you can't even say who you are? How dare you be so useless?"

It seems to me that I have screamed these words at the very top of my voice, but as soon as I have done so, my anger vanishes. I try to make myself breathe deeply, which is rather difficult as breathing is something else that I can't do here as I do in my world, but after a few moments, I am calmer.

"I shouldn't have said that," I say at last. "It was very rude of me. I was upset. I'm sorry."

I hang my head, my nose touching the sweet-smelling grass.

"Maya?"

The voice is gentler and kinder than ever.

"Yes?"

"After what's just happened, you're allowed to be a little bit cross. A little bit upset."

"Thank you," I reply politely.

"That's quite all right. Now, please don't mention it again. And anyway, it's not as though you're the first to say something like that. Plenty of people have before. Plenty will again, for that matter," it adds softly, almost as though to itself.

There's another pause before the voice speaks again. "Oh dear. This isn't really going according to plan."

"Well, that could be because we're not doing this right."

I haven't meant to say this: the words just seem to have emerged from me. I wonder yet again if I have offended the voice, but when it speaks next, it doesn't sound at all offended or annoyed but merely intrigued.

"What do you mean?"

I'm not at all sure what I do mean, but I am sufficiently encouraged by the voice's response to continue.

"Well," I say slowly, "perhaps instead of trying to guess everything, perhaps we should just see what we can actually do here. That way, perhaps we can work out what this—what being here, I mean—does. And if we can work out what being here does, we'll know what it's for."

"You mean because once you know what something is for, you can then usually decide what it is? Yes, I see. That's really very clever."

To my great surprise, the voice sounds genuinely impressed. I feel very pleased with myself, but then I remember my manners again.

"Thank you," I say, in what I hope is an appropriately modest tone. "Except perhaps asking what we can do isn't the right question either, because you and I can't do the same things. You can see and hear me, but I can only ever hear you. I can't see you. So perhaps you need to see me, and I don't need to see you."

"Or," says the voice slowly, "perhaps you need not to see—well, to see who you're talking to. I mean, perhaps it's important that you can't."

I am about to ask what the voice means when it speaks again.

"Well, all right. Let's start with you. What do you know you can do here?"

I turn again to look at the horses. It occurs to me that although I can't really look up, I can easily look down, and when I do, I find myself looking at the lower parts of my front legs, which are brown and black, just like Little Bran's. Then I realise that of course they are, we are sister and brother.

"I can see that Little Bran's got here all right and that he's happy here, far happier than he ever was in my world," I say to the voice. "So I can get Arlen to tell my parents that when I get back. That's quite important. Isn't it?"

"Yes, it is," it agrees emphatically. "Very important."

I look up again, or at least as well as I can, and this time I see nothing but the endless grass and the huge unbroken blue expanse above. All the horses have gone, which is just what I expected.

"And I don't see the horses any more," I go on slowly, "because I don't need to. And because I know that they're all here anyway."

"Yes. Like all the insects and birds and animals and people were, when we first met."

As I wait for the voice to continue, I swish my tail several times, not to dispel any flies—they are all here, just not in the way they so often are in my world—but because it feels nice, and I know that I won't have a tail for very much longer.

"So perhaps you're right," the voice carries on. "Perhaps you have come here to see that Little Bran's all right. Although it could be that what happened with Gorn meant that you got here faster. Then again, perhaps you also came here to find out a little more about who and what I am."

Suddenly, my impatience gets the better of me again.

"I really am very sorry I was so rude before. And I really don't mean to be rude now. But I don't understand why you always talk like this. Why can't you just say what you mean? Why can't you just tell me who, or what, you are?"

"Well," says the voice, sounding both a little surprised and ever so slightly reproving. "Perhaps you're being a little unfair there."

"Am I?" I ask, immediately feeling contrite again. "I'm sorry. I didn't mean to be."

"Oh, I'm sure you didn't," continues the voice. "But what I mean is that perhaps it's a little unfair to expect me to explain who I am when you don't know who you are."

"But I do know who I am," I reply, confused. "I'm Maya."

"Are you sure about that? We talked about this when we first met, don't you remember? When did you first decide that you were Maya? Did you decide the moment you were born? Or was it rather that first your mother and father, then Breccan and Rod, then Arlen, then everyone else, told you that that's who you are?"

It takes me quite a while to mull this over.

"Well, all right," I admit finally. "But I get to decide too. I mean, I might not agree that I'm who everyone says I am."

"No," says the voice. "You might not. But we talked about that, too, remember? How you add your own ideas of who you are to the ones other people have already given you? And how some ideas of who you are can be replaced by better ones? Isn't that what's happened to you? Ever since you and Arlen started seeing things that no one else could see? Isn't it true to say that you no longer agree with most other people's idea of who you are? But if that is true, it still doesn't mean that you yourself know who you are, does it? Which rather brings me back to what I said just now."

I don't know what to say to any of this.

"I'm sorry," the voice goes on, quickly but softly. "I do know how difficult this is."

It sighs. "I suppose that what I'm trying to say is that—"

Without meaning to, I suddenly find myself speaking again, finishing the voice's sentence.

"I've come here not to find out who you are but to find out who I am?"

The voice does not reply to this, but then I remember something else. "You said that this wasn't going to plan."

"Yes, I did say that, didn't I?" replies the voice, sounding sad. "And no. It certainly isn't."

The voice falls silent, and I know I will have to prompt it.

"Can I ask what your plan was, then?"

The voice seems to hesitate, almost as though plucking up the courage to say want it wants to say next.

"My plan," it says finally. "Yes, my plan." The voice stops and when it carries on again, its tone seems to be one of great reluctance. "Well, I suppose my plan was for the two of us, you and me, just to have a conversation. To talk about some important things. Not just about what you can now tell your parents about Little Bran. Although, as we said, that is important. But mainly about the wheat."

"The wheat?" I say, incredulous.

"Yes. The type of wheat that grows only on the Sea of Grass. The type where the seed pods don't open by themselves but wait to be picked. And what that has to do with the Lost Ones. Why it means you have to try and help them."

I still find the reference to the Lost Ones shocking, but much less so here than in my world. For a moment or two I am rather pleased by this, feeling that I must be more grown up than I had imagined. Then I realise this is not why the voice sounds reluctant.

"What else?" I ask, trying to fight down a rising sense of panic.

When the voice speaks again, its tone is quiet, matter-of-fact, and the most frightening I have ever heard it.

"To talk about Arlen and you. But I see now that I can't get you to understand what you need to know in a conversation. I need to tell you what's going to happen now. To the both of you."

I wake up the following morning, my head on Arlen's chest. As soon I realise where I am, I sit up and look at her.

"How long have I been gone?"

"Three days and three nights. How do you feel?"

I shake my head slightly. "You'd better tell me what's happened here. Not about Little Bran," I add quickly. "I already know what's happened. I know he's left."

Arlen hugs me and kisses the top of my head.

For a few moments, we sit in silence. Then Arlen begins telling me what happened from the moment I left.

She tells me that when Gorn attacked her, she cried out very loudly, and Karel's father Lato, who luckily had been making some arrowheads only a little way away, heard and ran over to see what was going on. It was his shout that I heard just before I went to speak with the voice.

"Lato said he got to me just in time," says Arlen. "Just in time to grab Gorn's wrist as he was trying to stab me. He said the most frightening thing wasn't that, but the expression on Gorn's face. He said Gorn looked as though he'd only just got started. And that he wasn't going to stop."

Arlen knows that I don't need her to explain what this means.

"Perhaps you were lucky to miss what happened next," she goes on after a few moments. "Ma, she—"

Arlen stops and swallows.

"I've never seen her so angry. She sent someone off to—well, some other Federation Councillors, I suppose, because the next day, two of them arrived here with one of the Law Sayers."

I gasp.

"A Law Sayer came here? To our village?"

"With two Federation Councillors." Arlen nods. "I've no idea how Ma got them to come. Anyway, she—The Law Sayer, I mean—wasn't here long. She went to the Elders first, and then she went to see your parents."

I frown, puzzled. "Why did the Law Sayer want to see my parents?"

Arlen shakes her head. "I don't know. Anyway, after she'd seen them, she spoke to Ma in private for quite a while. And then—" Arlen stops and swallows again.

"Then what?" I prompt her.

It's Arlen's turn to frown. "Well, I don't really know. Ma said that the Law Sayer advised first that everyone else—not just children, but everyone except Ma, the other Elders, the two Federation Councillors and a couple of other hunters—had to stay indoors. So I don't know what else the Law Sayer advised. But whatever it was, it only took half an hour or so. Then I poked my head out the door and saw Ma, the other two hunters—I couldn't make out who they were—and your Da take Gorn out to just beyond the ditch. After that, I couldn't see anything any more. It was too dark. So I didn't see what they did. But I heard all right. We all heard."

"Heard what?" I look up into Arlen's face and see that she looks faintly sick.

"Your Da told me. I could tell he didn't want to, but the noise was so awful, and they all knew we'd all heard it, so I suppose he felt he had to tell me."

Arlen takes a deep breath. "Ma told the two hunters and your Da to hold Gorn. To hold him really tight so he couldn't move, not at all. Then she took your Da's knife—you know, one of those long knives the hunters all have—and—"

She stops, and I have to prompt her again. "And what?"

"And she cut Gorn's belly open. All the way open. And then she reached inside it and pulled all his guts out."

She pauses, looking for the right words, then shrugs.

"Just pulled all his guts out," she repeats. "While Gorn was just standing there. They came out in great coils, your Da said. He said he was surprised by how much like a deer's guts they were. They just fell all over the ground and lay there with steam coming off them. And all the time, Gorn was screaming. We all heard him screaming. For such a long time. Then he was dead."

Arlen's eyes are blank for a moment, then she frowns and looks down at me. "You didn't—?"

Again, I am puzzled for a moment, but then I understand. I shake my head. "No. I didn't hear—I didn't feel—any of that."

Arlen lets out her breath. "Good. I wish I hadn't heard it."

"What will they do with him now?"

"I don't know." Arlen shivers.

We sit in silence for a little while with our arms around one another. Then I feel myself stiffen slightly. Arlen feels it as well.

"What is it?" she asks, concerned.

"There are some things that they have to know. Things that I saw and heard. When—when I was away."

Arlen hugs me tightly again. I bury my face in her hair and pull her even closer, wondering how long I will be able to bear this.

"Yes," she says. "I know there are."

"But I don't have to tell them everything," I add.

"No," agrees Arlen quickly. "Not everything."

I get to my feet and look down at her.

"When I was there, and when the voice spoke with me before, it asked me how I know that I'm me."

Arlen looks up, eyebrows raised. "What a funny question. And why did she ask it? She seems to know everything."

She looks away from me, which just now is a huge relief.

"No," I say. "She doesn't know everything. She's more or less told me as much. But she knows all about me. And all about us."

Arlen nods again. Then she shrugs. "She must do. How could she not?"

*

That evening, I go with Arlen and Serris to see my parents. Arlen tells them some of what happened to me after Gorn attacked her, about the grassland which wasn't the Sea of Grass, the huge herd of horses, the voice, and some of what the voice and I talked about. However, Arlen and I have already decided not to tell Serris and my parents anything else. It has never been easy for Arlen to talk to her mother about me, and she has always found it very hard even to mention my name to either of my parents. But although withholding information from them like this will make it even harder for her, she and I both feel that there is no choice. However, as it turns out, my father is too grief-stricken to pay much attention to what Arlen is saying, and Serris is so concerned for him and my mother that she doesn't spot the gaps in Arlen's account that normally she would see straight away.

When Arlen has finished, Serris takes her to my family's house, and as usual, I follow them. On our way there, Arlen whispers to me that my mother has been crying almost continuously since Little Bran left, but even with this warning, I am shocked by my mother's appearance. She is sitting with one hand clutching Edra to her, the other resting on the small bundle in Little Bran's hazel wand cot. Her unbound hair is hanging in lank grey strands around her white face, and she is making low wailing noises full of grief and misery.

I want to go to her and try physically to comfort her, but I know I can't. I bite my lip and look at Arlen, who in turn looks uncertainly at Serris.

After watching my mother for a few moments, Serris steps over to her and gently shakes her shoulder.

"Frey," she says. "Frey, look at me."

My mother looks up with the faintest of smiles, apparently still retaining some belief that Serris can help her cope with her despair. Serris takes my mother's face in her hands, wipes her tears away with her thumbs, smiles back at her and then gently kisses her on the mouth, once, then twice, then a third time.

Arlen and I watch, amazed: we are stunned not so much by seeing a tenderness which we have not previously suspected, more by it coming from one who only two days earlier gutted another living person with her own hands.

"Hush now," Serris says to my mother softly. "Hush now, just for a moment. Arlen has something she needs to tell you. Something about Maya. And about Little Bran."

Serris takes her hands from my mother's wet face and turns to look at Arlen. Slowly my mother does as well. Instinctively, I look round for Breccan or Rod. I don't see either of them, but then I hear Rod's whisper. "It's all right. Really." I feel him squeeze my arm. Then Arlen takes a deep breath and begins to speak.

"Maya went to a place where all the horses live. It might be the All Life, but she's not sure. Anyway, when Gorn attacked us, she was taken there. She told me. She doesn't know why. Not yet, anyway."

Arlen realises that she is speaking too quickly, so she stops and closes her eyes for a few moments. Although Serris, my parents, and even Edra are now all watching her, when she starts speaking again, she does so directly to my mother as though they are the only two people in the house.

"Maya described the place to me," Arlen goes on, now speaking slowly and clearly. "It's nice there. Really, really nice. Lots of grass—just grass I mean, no trees or anything, but not like the Sea of Grass, because there's no cold wind, and you're not afraid to look at the sky. And nothing but horses. Hundreds and hundreds of horses. Maya wasn't there for very long, but she saw Little Bran. She told me that that's the main reason she was taken there. Little Bran's now with the Horses, and he's decided to stay there, as one of them. He knew Maya and said hello to her. He's really happy, Maya could tell. Then after he'd said hello and let Maya know how happy he is, he went with the other horses, and they took him away with them." Arlen hesitates for a moment. "Then Maya came back here."

Everyone stares at her in silence. Then my mother, still with one arm around Edra, holds out the other to Arlen. Arlen steps over to stand beside her, and my mother holds her tightly. She has started crying again, but this time it's a lot quieter, and there doesn't seem to be quite so much pain in the sound.

*

Later that night, my father carries the small bundle to the Station. My mother, holding a torch in one hand and Edra's hand in the other, follows him. Breccan, Rod and I follow them a few paces behind. We have been walking in silence for only a few moments when Breccan touches my arm. I look up, and even in the dim light of my mother's torch, I can see the concern on his face. He leans down.

"They don't understand, do they?" he whispers urgently. "When you told them that Little Bran's going to stay there? With the Horses? That they won't ever see him again? Even when they come and—when they come for his—well, you know—"

Breccan falls silent. I know that he has always found it difficult to acknowledge the way in which he, Rod and I are different to other people. I have never really understood why.

Just as people differ from one another in the way they look, they can differ in the way they seem to other people to be in this world. It just so happens that Breccan, Rod and I did not stay in this world in the same way that people like Arlen, our parents and Edra stayed in it. Put more simply, we died: Breccan and Rod when they were three days old, and I just before my second birthday.

After we had died, each of us was taken on the journey to our Station, the same journey that Little Bran is being taken on now, carefully wrapped like him in tiny deerskin blankets. Once our bodies had been prepared by the insects and the birds, our skulls and other large bones—the enduring physical essence of what we had been in this world—were brought back from the Station to our home by our parents and placed carefully in the floor of our house by the front door, just as Little Bran's will be in about a year's time. That way, those who were close to us in this world will perhaps still be able to see, hear and speak with us, albeit not quite in the same way they do with other people more like themselves. However, whether they will actually do so is for people like Breccan, Rod, me and now Little Bran, to decide. This is because it is not a matter of how much those still confined to this world want to see and speak to those of us who are not, but how much they need to: and we are far better judges of that than they are.

I look into Breccan's anxious face and give him what I hope is a reassuring smile.

"No," I say. "They don't. It will be quite a while before they realise that Little Bran has decided to stay with the Horses in the All Life, or wherever it is, and that they'll never see or hear from him again. But that isn't important right now. Well, it isn't what's most important, anyway."

"Isn't it?" interjects Rod, looming into the torchlight from behind Breccan. "Then what is most important?"

I'm about to explain when I see them look past me towards our father. Turning, I see that he has removed the blankets and, with a gentleness we have not often seen in him, laid the tiny body onto the platform and is tying it down with rawhide strips. When he has finished, he pauses, then takes something else from the blanket and places it beside Little Bran. Although the light is feeble, I can see that it's Little Bran's rattle: we all call it that even though Little Bran never got to play with it. Then our father kneels, leans forward, his large, bearded face close to the tiny still one, and gives it the softest of kisses. He seems to hesitate. Then he strokes Little Bran's cheek several times before finally standing up and stepping back, only then wiping away the tears that have been steadily running down his nose and dripping off the end of it.

I turn back to my brothers.

"What's most important right now is that Ma and Da believe that they don't have to say goodbye to him forever."

Breccan glances at Rod, who nods. Then Breccan leans forward and envelops me in a huge hug. For a few moments, I'm too startled to say anything, and as soon as I try to ask him what the hug is for, Rod leans over to me and hugs me as well. When he lets me go, both he and Breccan smile at me. Then they turn, and each with one arm across the shoulder of the other, walk away. In a few moments, they have disappeared into the darkness. I will never see either of them again.

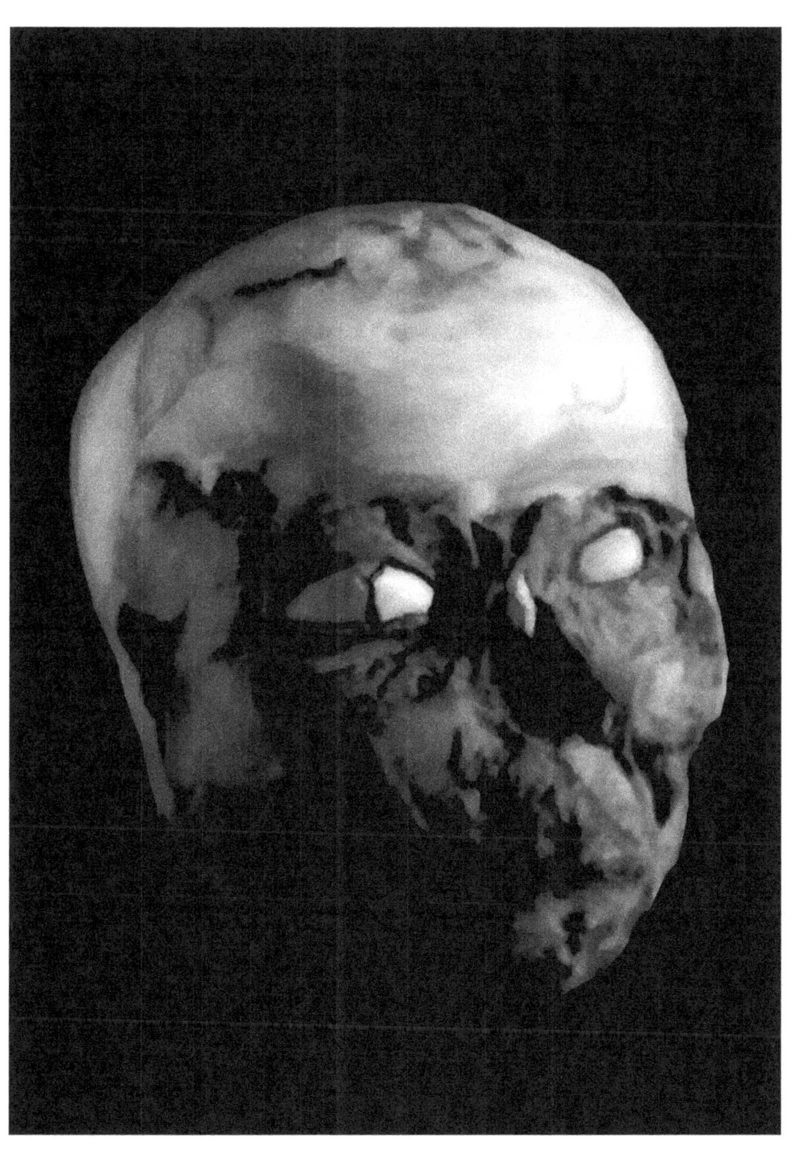

I will never hear the voice again either.

I didn't know this at the time, but even if I had, I wouldn't have minded, not after what it had told me about Arlen. As it is, I now know that she and I will have no more than a year together as we are before everything will change forever, so I want to spend as much of it with her as I can.

In the meantime, the trees are still being pushed back as the Sea of Grass continues to expand, and each year is colder and dryer than the one before. Food is scarcer than ever and even the youngest children have to become adept at trapping, fishing and foraging. The days are hard, and I spend each one waiting for Arlen to ask me what she needs to know and absolutely dreading it. But when it finally comes, it does so in a way that I would never have expected.

One day, Arlen suddenly asks old Emric if she can go with him to empty the fish traps instead of Efan, whose turn it is. Emptying the fish traps is a very odd sort of a job. It is undoubtedly a very important one, in that you need to be able to thank the fish properly so that they will agree to keep helping you, and you need to make sure that the quota isn't exceeded so that the village isn't fined on the advice of the Law Sayers. But since it also leaves you with red-raw hands and legs and feet so cold you can't feel them for quite a long time afterwards, it's also very unpopular, so no one ever volunteers for it. Old Emric is therefore a little taken aback when Arlen makes this offer, although he agrees readily enough.

When Arlen tells me what she has done, I begin to protest, although I can hardly explain why this is the last way in which I would want to spend the rest of my time with her. But then she says that we have to talk when we're not likely to be interrupted and that emptying the fish traps will give us the best chance of doing so. I realise that the time I have been so afraid of has finally arrived, and I agree without another word.

A few days later, the two of us are standing silently on Verba's banks with heads bowed while Emric talks to the fish before wading out to the fish traps. Emric knows all there is to know about the fish, and if the fact that the village almost always fills its quota is anything to go by, they clearly get on very well with him. He also made all the fish traps and all the willow nets himself, which would have been a huge amount of work, and he looks after them well. Everyone else is very grateful to him and genuinely admires him. But unfortunately, fish—what sort they are, where they live, what they eat, where they breed, which ones don't mind us taking them and which ones do—is the only thing he can ever talk about. So, although he has everyone's admiration and gratitude, he is nonetheless widely seen as the most terrible old bore. In view of what Arlen has to tell me, I am not expecting to care in the slightest about any of this. But despite that—or more likely because of it—we both find, as we are standing silently on Verba's bank watching Emric, knowing full well that his conversation with the fish is a very serious matter, that it is very hard indeed not to laugh.

However, by making sure that neither of us catches the other's eye, we just about manage to stay looking suitably solemn until finally Emric stops speaking to the fish and then says something to Verba. He stares into Verba's shallows for several long moments, then looks up at us.

"It's all right for you to come in," he says gravely.

With faces rigid, we murmur our own thanks to Verba and wade slowly out to where Emric is standing. He directs Arlen to a separate fish trap and then fusses over her for what seems like ages, repeating yet again what she is to look for, how to remove the fish, what to say to them and how to place them in the willow nets. Finally, and very grudgingly, he seems to accept that Arlen is not going to make any of the fish angry or wreck his precious trap, and he wades out to the larger fish traps in the deeper water.

Pretending to untie the willow twine securing the trap's lid, Arlen surreptitiously watches Emric go, then turns to me. She is just about to say something when she sees that several of our village's hunters have just emerged into view on Verba's far bank, on their way to wherever it is they're off to next. Karel is among them, the long hunter's knife he's now allowed to wear proudly displayed on his left thigh and the strange, curved wheat-gathering knife nowhere to be seen. For a moment, he gazes at Arlen with the most obvious longing. Although Arlen and I have never spoken about this, I know that she is well aware of how Karel feels about her and how ever since our relatively brief conversation on the wheat gathering expedition, he has tried to seek her out at every available opportunity, despite blushing furiously whenever he sees her, the blotches starting on his neck and then spreading all over his face.

Karel turns around now and waves. He really is a very sweet boy, and I know that Arlen is fond of him, as indeed am I. But she doesn't have anything like the same kind of feelings for him that he so clearly has for her. In fact, she is growing increasingly exasperated by Karel's yearning. It is against the Law for any couple from the same village to marry, so Arlen considers that Karel should both try a little harder to control himself and be a little more accepting of the sheer impossibility of anything ever happening between the two of them, at least of the kind he obviously wants so much to happen.

I'm therefore a little taken aback when on seeing Karel wave to her, Arlen thrusts her arm up and out of the water, showering her and me with droplets, and waves back at him, smiling in what looks like absolute delight. Karel, surprised but plainly elated, smiles back, his teeth showing white in his soot-darkened face. For a moment, in which I feel as though someone has just thrust a spear into me, he looks happier than I have ever seen him before. But then one of the other hunters says something to him. He turns quickly, and within a few moments he has disappeared into the trees with the other hunters. The happy smile on Arlen's face slowly fades and is replaced by a quite inscrutable expression. Then she looks at me.

"Well?" she says, a little defiantly. "That's what you want, isn't it?"

Then the defiance vanishes, and she smiles again. "Anyway, what do you expect? Obviously, I'm Becoming a Woman."

Nearly every girl our age has heard these words from their mothers at one time or another and always spoken in this terribly serious way. Arlen laughs, and I do too, partly with genuine amusement but mostly with relief at dispelling of the tension. However, Arlen's laughter is too loud for Emric, who looks up at her, harpoon poised in mid-air and clearly very annoyed.

"Oi," he hisses at her. "Be quiet."

Arlen promptly straightens her face and readdresses herself to the fish trap. But then Emric hisses at her again.

"I don't know what you're laughing at," he says, still sounding very angry. "There's nothing funny about fish, you know."

For a few seconds, Arlen just about manages to keep her lips pressed together. But she cannot stifle a loud snigger through her nose, and then she bursts out laughing, dropping the lid of the fish trap into the water. Still laughing, she scrabbles for it but wobbles, loses her footing on the slippery rocks, flails her arms for a moment, and then with a loud splash, falls onto her backside in the shallow water.

"Whoops," she gasps out, as well as she can for laughing. "Oh no. Oh dear."

She just sits there, up to her chest in the water, laughing helplessly. Emric looks furiously at her and this time yells at her at the top of his voice. "What are you doing, girl? You're upsetting all the fish."

Arlen looks towards him and attempts to speak, but instead just gasps. I can tell that she is trying to say sorry to Emric, but I can also see that she's now laughing so hard she can't get any actual words out, which by itself is making her laugh even more, the tears starting from her eyes. Emric glares at her in impotent rage, then yells at her again.

"Go on, just get out of here."

I wade over to Arlen, grasp her arm, pull her upright and lead her, still helpless, to the bank. Although Arlen's laughter is making me laugh as well, there is something about it I find faintly worrying, so I am relieved when, just as we reach Verba's grassy bank, she calms down a little.

Gently, she shakes me from her, stoops to cup some of Verba in her hands and with an apology to him, splashes it over her face. Then she allows me to help her out and onto his bank, and we walk quickly downstream.

After a short time, we arrive at a spot just by a still pool that we both know well. I help Arlen pull off her soaking clothes and she spreads them out on the rocks so that the small patch of sunlight can dry them a little. Then, completely naked, she steps over the still pool of Verba's water and gazes down into it. After a few moments, but without looking up, she beckons me to join her. I realise what she wants to do, and I hesitate. Arlen beckons again impatiently.

"It's been so long since we've done this," I say, stepping reluctantly over to her and looking down into the still water.

Arlen doesn't reply at first, but just continues to gaze at our reflections. I feel awkward and carry on talking in what I know perfectly well is a weak attempt to cover the fact.

"I know Emric's completely humourless. But I don't know why you had to laugh at him like that. We could get into a lot of trouble."

Arlen gives a soft but derisive grunt. "Oh come on. There's nothing funny about fish. Really."

Still not looking up from the pool, she puts one arm around my waist, and as she pulls me close to her, I notice something.

"You feel different," I say.

"Do I now?" Arlen replies in an innocent-sounding tone. "Different in what way?"

I reach round her waist, gently stroking her belly, then reach down to her right thigh.

"I don't know. You feel softer. It's nice, though."

"That's probably something to do with the fact that I've begun to bleed," says Arlen casually, still not looking up. "To bleed as all women used to bleed when they got to this age, I mean. Apparently, I'm the first girl in thirty generations to do so."

I take my arm from around her waist as though she is suddenly too hot to touch, and stand there gaping at her in stunned silence. After a few moments, Arlen finally looks up at me and smiles again. Then she reaches out and puts her arm around my waist. As she squeezes me gently, she leans towards me and whispers in a mock-conspiratorial tone.

"But you already knew that, Maya. My friend. My oldest, closest friend. Didn't you?"

I want to speak, but I am still unable to do so. This would be so much easier if Arlen began to shout and scream and to hit me. Instead, she suddenly laughs softly and squeezes me again.

"It's all right. No, really. It is. Come on now. If this is going to work, we need to do it properly. Then perhaps you'll understand rather better."

She lets go of me and squats down, once again studying the still water. Realising that there is no point in resisting any further, I do the same. The sun is now quite low, so the light is just about right. I stare down at what I know to be my own face. Although I am still in shock from what Arlen has just said, I try to concentrate on not looking at the reflection of Arlen's face right next to the reflection of mine, and instead try to find the little things about my own face that she has so often described to me. I search for the yellow spots in my brown eyes, the freckles across my nose, the small pale birthmark near my jawline. Of course I have never been able to make these out in my reflection in this pool or in any other one, and I never will: I know they are there only because Arlen has so often told me they are. But it is only by searching intently for them that what I am really looking for will start to appear, and after only a few moments, it does.

As I gaze at the reflection in Verba, my face becomes Arlen's, just as Arlen's face becomes mine. As I have said to her, it has been a long time since she and I have done this. But it is the kind of thing that always seems familiar, no matter how long it has been since you did it last. But then something quite unexpected happens. The reflected face at which I'm staring in the still water—Arlen's face, the tiniest detail of which I know so well—begins to change. It is growing older as I watch it. Then something makes me look at the face next to the one I am studying, and I see that it's the face of a very young child.

In all the times that Arlen and I have done this, I have never seen anything like this, and for a moment I feel a rising panic, a sense that everything everywhere is terribly wrong. Then the panic becomes pain, and the pain makes me want to scream, to shout out against the huge, monstrous unfairness of it, but I can't make any sound at all. I sit back, my head tilted upwards. I shut my eyes as tightly as I can, but even so, I cannot stop the tears leaking out, running down past my ears and into my hair. When finally I open my eyes again, I look up and see how far the sun has moved: we have been at the pool for over an hour. I turn to Arlen, and finally find my voice.

"Why?"

Still smiling, Arlen proceeds to tell me.

*

Three nights earlier, Arlen suddenly wakes up. Although she doesn't need to urinate, she can feel something leaking out of her. She gets up from her bed and reaches down between her thighs. As she feels the blood slick beneath her fingers, there is a pricking in her chest, getting sharper and sharper until it feels like she is being stabbed with hundreds of tiny needles. She begins to gasp, but she can't seem to get nearly enough air into her lungs. Then her throat begins to tighten, and her heart starts to pound as though it is trying to beat its way out of her chest.

Arlen is about to begin screaming for me when she feels her mother's arms go around her. Instinctively understanding that Arlen needs to be outside, Serris helps her get dressed and then, with Arlen gripping her wrists in her own bloody hands, she leads her through the door of their house and into the cold night air. There, Serris makes Arlen sit down until she begins breathing more normally, but as soon as she does so, Serris realises that her daughter is drenched in sweat. Arlen begins to shake again, but this time with cold. Serris goes back into the house, returning moments later with a large, otter pelt blanket which she wraps around Arlen's shoulders before hugging her close again. Arlen asks her where I am, but Serris does not answer her.

150

They sit like this for what seems like hours, Serris taking her arms from Arlen only once to pick up a stone to throw at a big rat that looks as though it wants to dart into the house. Arlen cannot remember her mother ever holding her like this before.

When at last it starts to get light, Arlen looks down and sees for the first time that she has been sitting in a large pool of her own congealing blood. She starts up with a cry of dismay and disgust but again, Serris holds her firmly, then gently raises her to her feet. Slowly, she lifts Arlen's clothing and, using several hand-fuls of damp moss, wipes her clean before deftly tying what feels to Arlen like soft strips of hide onto her. Then they walk slowly over to my house, Serris telling Arlen that my mother will help look after her, as she has so many times before. Of course, Arlen expects me to be there. But again, I am not.

My mother is preparing breakfast for herself and Edra, but the moment she sees Serris and Arlen, she stops. She then looks at Serris with the same expression of uncertainty and apprehension that we have both seen so often in these last few weeks, but this time also with what looks like grief. My mother asks Serris whether it has happened, and Serris nods. Then, ignoring Arlen's demands to tell her where I am, Serris and my mother lead Arlen back to her own house, where they proceed to tell her what is happening to her.

Serris explains that Arlen is bleeding in the way that once, all women bled and that she is the first girl in thirty generations to do so in any village in any of the Federations. For a time, Arlen does not understand what her mother has just said to her, so Serris has to repeat it several times. Then, when the initial shock has finally subsided a little, Arlen demands to know how and why. Serris then tells her that this is because ever since Arlen was five years old, she has been given better food than anyone else in the entire Federation. Not only has she had some of the best fatty meat from every single kill, no matter how scarce, but mar-row and even some precious brain has been put into almost every meal that Frey has given to her. Serris tells Arlen that my mother's skill in disguising the content of Arlen's meals in this way was in fact one of the main reasons that Arlen has so often eaten in our house rather than her own.

Arlen is even more shocked to hear this than she was to be told why she has begun bleeding, but then the questions start pouring out. How, she asks her mother, could Frey get hold of the best fatty meat, to say nothing of marrow and brain, without any of the other hunters knowing? What will happen when the hunters find out that this has been going on for years? How will Bran react when he discovers that his own wife has been betraying him and everyone else in the village in this way? What will the Federation Council say about such wickedness? What punishment will the Law Sayers advise?

But then Arlen sees that instead of being alarmed at the prospect of my father, the other hunters and the Federation Council finding out what they have done, Serris and my mother simply looked puzzled. Then Serris seems to realise something, and she shakes her head impatiently.

No, no, she says to Arlen. You don't understand. It was never a question of the hunters and the Federation Council finding out. They all knew about it from the very beginning. Because it was all done according to a plan that both the Council of the Western Federation and the Supreme Council had already approved.

Again, Serris has to repeat this to Arlen at least twice, and even then, it is a long time before Arlen can begin to make enough sense of what she has just been told to ask whose plan this was. At this point, Serris and my mother look at each other for a very long time. Finally, it is my mother who answers.

The Traveller, she says. It was the Traveller's plan.

My mother goes on to explain how Serris first learnt of this plan when she went to seek the Traveller's advice as to which of our former Federation's villages had to leave it.

The Traveller had told Serris that even though we were now able to hunt on the Sea of Grass, food resources overall were continuing to dwindle, so that if we continued as we were, all the world would starve in less than five generations. There was, the Traveller had said, only one hope of averting this disaster.

The Traveller knew—she did not tell Serris how—that soon, two girl children would be born into Serris' own village, within days of one another. One of these children would be weak and sickly and would, within only a couple of years of her birth, apparently leave the world and join her two elder brothers in the All Life. But in fact, the true essence of this child would for a while not merely stay in this world but would join with that of the other child, so that the two would be one. And this child, said the Traveller, being now two children in one—one being solely in this world, and the other being both in this world and in the All Life—would be able to see things in both worlds at the same time, which not even the Traveller Herself could do. This was the slender hope of averting disaster, said the Traveller. In being able to see things both in this world and in the All Life simultaneously, this child—the child who was two children—might be able to see a way in which people in this world could yet survive.

It would in fact be through this ability to see things that others could not see that this child would unwittingly identify herself. The moment she did so, the Traveller had said, every possible measure would have to be taken to ensure that she would survive and, for a short time at least, thrive. This would mean not merely protecting the child from harm but giving her the best possible food. That was why the Move had to happen. The child could only be given the best food if her village left the Northern Federation, in which, being closest to the Sea of Grass, the food shortage was most acute, and joined the Western Federation. The Traveller knew that the Council of the Western Federation would accept Her advice that our village should join it and that having done so, would then have no choice but to give Her secret plan its backing.

At this point, although she is feeling dazed at the strangeness of all she has been told, Arlen is struck by the way both her own mother and mine refer to the Traveller. The subject of the Traveller does not often come up in everyday conversation, but whenever it does, She is always referred to in deeply respectful, even awestruck tones. By contrast, Serris and my mother have spoken of Her with undisguised bitterness. Arlen asks Serris why this is so, especially since Serris was once so favoured by the Traveller.

Serris looks at Arlen for a few moments, her expression inscrutable. Then she laughs a short, derisive laugh.

Oh yes, she says, her voice harsh with sarcasm. Favoured. Favoured by being allowed to visit the Traveller, by staying with Her for two whole days, because she was the only one to have guessed the meaning of the message that the Traveller had brought back from Her visit to the Animals of the Sea of Grass three years before, the message about using the animals' own brains. But, Serris adds, there's just one problem with this famous story. It's a lie.

Serris had no more idea than anyone else what the message from the Animals of the Sea of Grass meant. She had never asked the Trader Gello to pass a message to the Council of the Northern Federation about it. It was the Traveller who had told Gello to pass a message to Serris.

It was a very complicated and very secret message, the kind only a Trader could be relied upon to convey precisely and with complete discretion. The Traveller's message told Serris exactly what she was to say, to whom she was to say it, and when. It told her how she was to inform the Elders of her village that she had guessed the meaning of the message, how she was to insist that this be relayed to the Supreme Council, how she was then to insist on being taken to see the Traveller, and how she was to carry on insisting on these things, no matter what she was threatened with and how frightened these threats made her. So in those two days that the Traveller and Serris spent together, it had not been Serris explaining the meaning of the message from the Animals of the Sea of Grass to the Traveller. It had been the Traveller explaining it to Serris.

There is another long silence. Finally, Arlen asks Serris why, if the Traveller already knew what this message meant, did She pretend to everyone, except this insignificant young woman, that She did not? What was the point of such an elaborate trick? And why did she choose Serris to help Her play it?

But at this point, Serris falls silent. So it is again my mother who explains to Arlen that Serris had asked the Traveller precisely those questions, but that the Traveller had never given any answer. It was, said my mother, as though the Traveller had lost interest. It was not until much later that both my mother and Serris realised that this was precisely what had happened. The Traveller was indeed no longer interested in the subject.

After all, my mother goes on, sounding angrier than Arlen has ever heard her, would you bother to explain to the tool you've just made what you want that tool to do? Of course you wouldn't. You simply use the tool for whatever needs doing, and when it's done, you forget about it until you need it again.

Because, Serris interrupts, that is what people are to the Traveller. Nothing but tools. The Traveller sees people in exactly the same way that anyone else might see a scraper or a digging stick. Or a knife, she adds after a moment, now sounding even angrier than my mother. A knife that you might need for a particularly messy, nasty piece of butchery that once done, you'd really rather forget about. To the point where you'd rather not see that knife again because you don't want to be reminded of the horrible thing you had to do with it.

Hearing these last words, Arlen begins to realise that all that she has heard so far is just a prelude to what her mother and mine have yet to tell her, and that all the shocks she has received are nothing compared to the true horror yet to come. Her stomach seems to sink, her neck, face and scalp are suddenly covered in a clammy sweat, and she feels as though she is about to be sick. She wants to ask Serris exactly what she means, but when she tries to speak, no words come out. Seeing this, Serris tells her in a few short simple sentences what Arlen suddenly knows to be the truth.

This is that Arlen and I were the reasons not only for the Move, but for the Massacres that the Move then helped make possible, and that all the men, women and children in all those villages in the Southern Federation that were destroyed when she and I were very young were slaughtered because of us.

Yet when Arlen speaks, she is rather surprised to hear that her voice is calm and measured, even polite. She asks Serris to tell her exactly how she and my mother came to be mass murderers.

Serris flinches at the words, but after a few moments, gathers herself again and resumes her explanation.

The Traveller had not been satisfied with my mother's and Serris' mere agreement to do all they could to put the Traveller's plan into effect, but had insisted that they both swear by the All Life, which they did. Only then did the Traveller tell them that the child's continued survival would mean that the day would come when she might be able to see a way in which people could yet avoid starvation. What the Traveller never told them was that the only way this child's continued survival could be accomplished was by arranging for the deaths of as many of her competitors for food as possible.

It seems to Arlen that Serris and my mother do their very best to make her believe that they tried everything to avoid coming to this terrible conclusion. Serris even sent my father to the Traveller in one last attempt to seek an alternative. But all She would tell him was that whilst She would facilitate whatever way Serris and my mother devised for fulfilling their unbreakable oath, the responsibility for fulfilling it lay with them.

So Serris and my mother prepared their dreadful proposals and my father relayed them to the Traveller. Somehow, although Serris tells Arlen that she has never known how, the Traveller procured the tacit approval of an appalled but compliant Supreme Council. My father, having been made Federation Hunt Master through the intervention of the Traveller years before, was of course perfectly placed to implement these proposals. And so, with a handful of other hunters, all of whom had in one way or another been similarly compromised by the Traveller, he began the vile work.

Arlen has difficulty hearing whatever else Serris and my mother tell her because of the swirling confusion in her head, in which she feels as though she can hear someone speaking in a voice just too faint for her to hear, trying to explain something that she knows must be very important. But it seems that somehow, she does hear it, because a few days later, she remembers what it is.

*

"It was my anger that stopped me hearing and understanding straight away," says Arlen, stroking my hair. "Which is funny, really. Because if I'd understood straight away what I needed to do now, I wouldn't have been angry in the first place."

"What do you mean? What is it you need to do?"

Arlen smiles as though she is indulging me, which in a way, she is.

"I need to die, of course. Don't you see that I've no alternative? Your mother and mine are still bound by their oath to the Traveller. Their oath to protect me, no matter what. The only way they could see to fulfil it was to murder hundreds and hundreds of people. They did so, but still, there is less and less food. Now that I know what they've done, how can I just wait for them to decide that they have to do it again?"

She looks at me and seeing that I'm still unable to speak, carries on.

"And anyway, it's what I want. I don't want to stay here, not like this. I can't be the living reason that all those people died. I can't carry on, knowing that they were murdered for me, that I am the reason for all that pain and misery. I'm ready to go. And by midwinter, I'll have gone."

"And me?" I blurt out, hating my selfishness and the petulance in my voice but unable to control either. "What about me? I'm nothing without you."

Arlen shuts her eyes, puts her head back, and laughs softly.

"You really couldn't be more wrong about that."

From that day on, Arlen cannot eat or drink anything. She tells Serris and my mother—she cannot bring herself to speak to my father—that there is nothing to be done. Even if food or drink were forced into her, she says, her body would reject it. At first, all three assume that it is because Arlen is still in shock from what Serris and Frey have told her, and then once it becomes clear that this is not the explanation, they assume that Arlen is making some kind of protest. Finally, however, they realise that Arlen's explanation—that she cannot bear to stay as she is any longer—is the simple truth, and that there is nothing they can do about it. Soon, Arlen cannot leave her house, and a few days after that, she goes into a coma. Three days before the Midwinter Solstice, the Arlen I have known finally leaves, and for the first time ever, I am utterly alone.

I couldn't question the justice of Arlen's decision then, and have never been able to do so since. But although this all happened in a very different time, I still find that just talking about it is almost impossibly painful. I know that I have to tell you because again, if I don't, nothing from this point on is likely to make much sense. And I suppose it might also help explain what I told you when we first began, about how so many people assume that they know me. They don't seem to understand that no one could ever share another person's grief and sorrow without having experienced their own, and that if someone seemed to have an infinite capacity to absorb pain, it would mean only that they never actually felt it at all. Or rather, people could understand it if they wanted to, but they very much want not to: as I said at the beginning, if people really don't want to believe something, they won't, no matter how obviously true it is.

Yet I can't help wondering what people like this would say if they knew how often I have wished that just for an hour, I could once again be that young girl, back in the safety of the trees, lying in my friend's arms. If, for just for that single hour, I could forget about looking after everyone and feel that someone was looking after me.

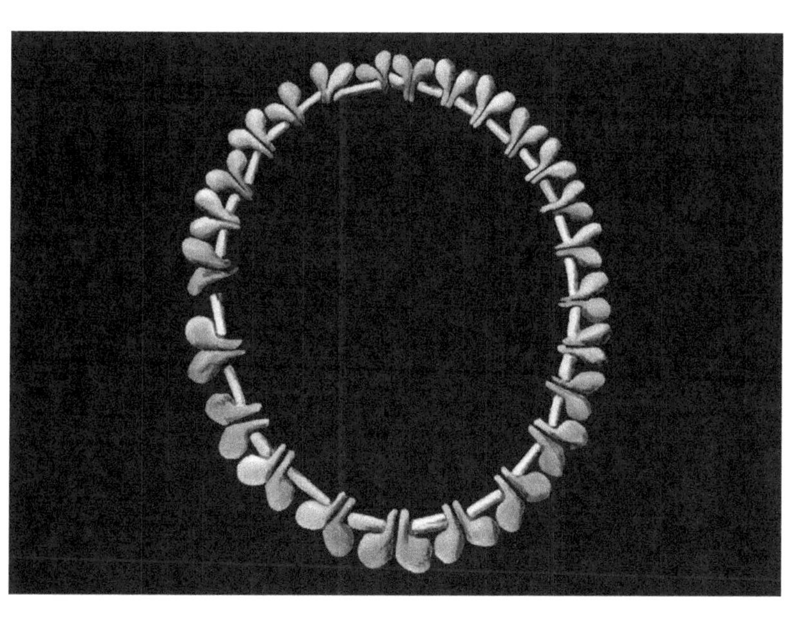

Only a week after Arlen leaves, a messenger arrives from the Council of the Western Federation. Standing just outside our village's perimeter ditch, she declaims the news that the White Plague is walking once again, this time in the villages of the Eastern Federation.

Until further notice is received from the Law Sayers, the Quarantine Law comes into force with immediate effect. All travel of any kind must cease except to gather food, and that is permitted only once a day, between sunrise and sunset, by a group of no more than three adults to be accompanied at all times by one of the hunters whose bow will ensure that no one else comes closer than fifty paces. The remaining hunters, including my father, take it in turns to patrol the village ditch. Any person attempting to leave or enter the village without permission will be challenged and risks being shot, regardless of their identity.

But this time, the Quarantine Law seems to make little difference, and once again, the White Plague takes several from our village. Then, on the night of the third day after the Quarantine Law has come into force, Edra rushes into Serris' house shortly after sunrise. She tells her that our mother has been coughing in the night and is now missing, leaving flecks of blood covering the hide and bracken on her bed. Serris follows her outside, but then Edra catches sight of our mother in the distance, well beyond the village ditch and walking unsteadily towards the tents that have been put up about two hundred paces beyond it. With a scream, she leaves Serris and runs after her, but before she can cross the ditch, her arm is gripped, and she is pulled backwards. Cador, an arrow already nocked on his bowstring, shakes his head. He waits until Serris and I are closer then speaks to Edra.

"She said you'd try and follow her," he says. "She asked me to stop you."

Furiously, Edra tries to pull her arm free from Cador's grasp, but he's far too strong for her.

"Let me go," she screams at him, over and over.

Without exerting himself, Cador maintains his grip on Edra's arm but then suddenly releases it just as she tries again to wrench it from him, and she nearly falls over. The surprise of doing so seems to shake her, and she makes no further attempt to get past Cador. He looks at her pityingly, then sighs.

"Your Ma asked me to stop you when you tried to run after her. And I have."

He steps to one side and nods his head in the direction of the tents.

"You can go after her now if you want to," he continues. "But if you do, you can't come back. If you try, you'll be shot. Either I'll shoot you, or one of the others will. I'm sorry, but there it is. Are you sure that's what you want?"

I look to where he has gestured and see that Serris has walked back to join Mira and Lind. Mira has grown very close to Edra over the last few months and is now watching her, terror-stricken. Lind is sitting on the ground at Serris' feet, hugging herself and weeping silently. Suddenly, Edra's body seems to sag. Without another word to Cador, she walks slowly back to Mira. They both sit down next to Lind and put their arms around her, heads touching.

After that, we are permitted to take a little food once each day to a point a hundred paces beyond the village ditch, cover it with large stones to protect it from the animals, then return to the ditch to see who comes to collect it. Old Dara is the last one to go to the tents. One morning a week after that, the stones covering the food left the previous evening are still undisturbed, and we know that the White Plague has finally moved on.

We wait the further three days required by the Quarantine Law and then we go to them. Serris, Bran and I find Frey in one of the tents: she and Dara have clearly been the last. The foxes and rats have been busy, and most of her face and her right hand are already gone. However, she is still wearing the snail shell necklace my father gave her when they were first married and which she must have put on just before she went to the tents so that we would know her.

Serris kneels beside the body and is still for several moments before leaning forward to smell its hair. Then she puts out an arm towards Bran, and he takes it and helps her back to her feet. She wipes the tears from her face, then bends down again and begins removing the cloak and tunic from the body so that she and my father can put it into the special clothes for its journey to the Station.

Suddenly, Serris stops, peering at something. Without taking her eyes from whatever she has seen, she reaches out again to Bran and touches his arm. He has just been staring helplessly at the body, and at Serris' touch, he starts.

"What? What is it?"

"Her left hand," Serris answers quietly, nodding towards it. "Look."

Bran stoops to do so, as do I. The fingers of the left hand are tightly closed into a fist as though gripping something very tightly, and there are several thin strips of rawhide knotted around the hand itself. After a gesture from Serris, Bran reaches into the pouch on his belt and pulls out a small scraper, with which he cuts carefully through the rawhide strips one by one. When he has removed them—there are five in all—he and Serris prise the rigid fingers apart and stare at what is in the now-open hand: several dried stalks of grass, including ears comprising ripe yet intact seed pods.

"Wheat?" whispers Bran after several moments, both looking and sounding incredulous.

Serris frowns. "Yes." She reaches down to pick up the dry stalks, which are clearly very delicate. She straightens up again, holding her hand out and open so that Bran and I can see the contents up close. We both recognize it straight away.

"It's from the Sea of Grass," whispers Bran. "The kind where the pods just wither without opening."

Serris nods. "The kind that Arlen and Maya wanted to talk about when they brought it back all those years ago. The kind that they found so interesting without being able to say why. And not just that. Look."

She holds up the ends of the stalks closer to Bran's face. He peers at them, then grunts.

"They've been cut."

Serris nods again and places the stalks carefully onto Bran's palm. Then she looks down again at the now limp hand, the marks of the rawhide strip clear upon it.

"And there. Look. She must have bound up this hand with her other one. As though she needed to protect what she had in it. As though she needed to make sure that nothing would get to it until I—until we—"

Her voice trails off as she gazes at what little is left of the face. But Bran is still staring at the wheat stalks in his hand as though they are the strangest things he has ever seen.

"But where did she get it?" he demands suddenly. "The last wheat gathering party was, what, two weeks before the Autumn Equinox? And what was she holding it for? Some sort of sign?" He looks down again at the body. "If it is, I don't understand it."

He turns, frowning, to Serris. "Do you?"

Serris shakes her head slowly, suddenly looking very old. Then she turns to Bran and with a sad smile, puts her hand up to his face and strokes it gently.

"I'd like to be alone with her for a little while. Not for long. Is that all right?"

Bran looks at Serris intently for a moment, then takes her small hand in both of his very large ones and nods. Without another word, he turns and leaves the tent.

As I watch him go, it occurs to me that somehow, he is not my father. I quickly turn back again to the body and have a similar feeling: that was not my mother. Then Serris kneels down again, and as she once more leans over to smell Frey's hair, I understand.

Serris closes her eyes and leans back again. She smiles and, her eyes still shut, half-turns her head in my direction.

"Arlen," she says quietly. "I wondered if you'd be here."

"Of course I am, mother," I reply. "You need me. So here I am."

I can still remember that odd feeling—a curious combination of shock, surprise and, to be honest, delight—that I felt on realising that I was now Arlen and that I would never be just Maya again. I've never really understood why I should have felt this way because frankly, after all that had happened, it should have been obvious. My Arlen might be gone forever, but that had nothing whatever to do with Serris' desperate need for her Arlen's understanding of what she had done, even if there was no prospect of obtaining her actual forgiveness. Nor was Karel's intense longing for his Arlen very likely to waste away as Arlen's body had. But I have to admit that I was very surprised to find out how many other people needed their versions of Arlen as well.

I first begin to realise this when news of the discovery of the wheat in Frey's hand—I have already lost all sense of her and Bran as my parents, although oddly enough, it is not being replaced by any real feeling of Serris as my mother—starts to spread. Everyone guesses that it is some kind of message, a very important message. But just like the famous message from the Animals of the Sea of Grass all those years before, no one can work out what it actually means.

After a few days, Lato asks Serris if she will convene a meeting of the Elders, with a view to asking the Council of the Western Federation itself to consider something that has not been done in very many years—seeking the advice of the Traveller.

Serris has been rather listless since Frey's departure, but this request annoys her so much that suddenly, she is almost her old self again and sends poor Lato away with a stinging rebuke. When the next day, Karel comes to tell her that he will be going to seek the Traveller's advice and that I will be going with him, he fares even worse.

"What are you talking about, you stupid boy?" Serris barks at him. "I've already said that we are not requesting any decision from the Council. And anyway, you know perfectly well that it's not for you just to stroll off to see the Traveller whenever you feel like it—" She stops in mid-tirade as she realises just what Karel has said.

"What do you mean, Arlen will be going with you?" she asks him in a quite different tone of voice.

Karel has flushed a deep red, clearly very angry at Serris' rudeness, and is just about managing to control himself.

"Please forgive me, madam" he replies, his demeanour as formal as his actual words. "I see that I have put that rather badly. I do not mean that this is something that I have decided. What I mean is that it is something that your daughter has decided and that she has told me of her decision."

From where I am sitting, I can see Serris stiffen, although somehow, she manages to stop herself from turning around to look at me. Fortunately, Karel is so preoccupied with his own anger that he doesn't notice.

"I see," Serris says after a long pause. "You do realise that the Supreme Council and the Law Sayers are likely to have something to say about that?"

Karel flushes an even deeper red. He tries to speak, coughs, clears his throat and tries again. "That, madam, is almost exactly what I said to your daughter. She replied that that will depend on what the Traveller says."

Serris stares at him and then sighs. "Yes. I suppose it will." Then she collects herself. "Very well," she says briskly. "When are you leaving?"

Karel hesitates, frowning. "I am not sure. Your daughter was—well, she wasn't quite so clear about that."

He purses his lips and shrugs as though making it clear that there is nothing more he can add. Serris stares at him for a moment or two longer, then nods.

"It's all right," she says and smiles at Karel. "I understand," she adds. "Really, I do."

Karel smiles an awkward smile back at her.

"And I'm sorry I was so very rude to you just now," Serris goes on. "I'm still a little upset, you see. Do please forgive an old woman's foolishness."

"Of course, madam," Karel replies, bowing again, even more stiffly than before. He turns and leaves hurriedly.

The moment Karel is out of sight, the smile leaves Serris' face. "Stupid boy," she repeats, although this time to herself. Then she turns around to face me. "Well, well, my daughter. You really are full of surprises, aren't you?"

I shrug. "If I am, mother, I have you to thank."

*

When I first mentioned to Karel that he and I were going to visit the Traveller, I assumed that this would be within the next few months. In fact, we will not go for very many years.

I have already decided that if I am going to be a part of Karel's life in a way he never really expected, he and I are going to have to do a lot of talking. So at first, that is all we really do.

For the first few years, our discussions are a little difficult because there are so many things that either worry Karel or which he finds very hard to understand. He worries that his conversations with me will make everyone else treat him differently. There is no point in my trying to persuade him that this isn't so—I know it is, and he knows I know—so I have to try and persuade him that this is something to which he will become accustomed. Understandably perhaps, Karel is rather sceptical about this, at least at first. He points out that whereas I grew up with Maya and have no real memory of a time when she was not with me, he as an adult is having to get used to me in a wholly new way. Finally, however, he sees that whether he grows accustomed to it or not, there isn't any alternative.

What he finds hard to understand is why I can't simply tell him what it is that he and everyone else need to know. Finally, I hit upon a way of explaining this by getting Karel to recall something that Bran had told him and all the other young men on their first day as hunters.

Bran had explained that learning wasn't simply a matter of an older, experienced hunter telling a younger inexperienced one how to do everything, whether it was making a new bow, tracking a wounded deer or finding water on the Sea of Grass. That was obviously a part of it, but Bran had explained that the far more important part was the younger men watching the older men do all these things, and bit by bit, gaining the confidence to ask themselves whether there was anything about what they were watching that might perhaps be done better. At first, Karel and his fellow students hadn't believed this. Surely, one of them had said, experience would always beat inexperience. Of course, it would, Bran had replied. It would beat it every time. But experience of what? Experience of, say, finding a good campsite? Or experience of learning how to find a good campsite? If it was the second, which of the two—the older men or the younger—had the more recent experience? And then the younger men understood.

From this point on, Karel and I make better progress. It is not before time. The Massacres from when Maya and I were young and then the visit of the White Plague has made the food shortage less acute, but it is still bad enough. The continued spread of the Sea of Grass soon results in the Northern Federation being dissolved, the land on which its villages once stood amongst the trees now just another part of the empty grassland. The villages of the former Northern Federation have to be absorbed into the remaining three, most migrating to the still-rebuilding Southern Federation, and the nomads of the eastern and southern deserts with whom we once traded have long since disappeared. Unless something else changes, it will not be that long before all people are gone from this world forever.

*

In due course, Serris and then Bran leave and return to the All Life. So far as I am aware, neither is seen in this world again. This is probably because everyone close to them here, apart from me, have either already gone on ahead of them or moved away, like Edra, who marries a boy from a village in the Eastern Federation. In fact, in what seems to me a very short period, nearly everyone who Maya and I grew up with has gone, except for Karel.

Yet still I have no idea of what the sign of the cut wheat in

167

Frey's hand means. I am waiting for something to happen, waiting for some clue to tell me what I need to do. Then, far, far later than it should have done, it occurs to me that I have forgotten the very lesson I taught Karel years earlier. It is no good just waiting for the answers to come to me. I must go in search of them.

Karel has long since stopped asking me when we are going to see the Traveller and has in fact quite forgotten that I ever told him that that was what we were going to do. By now he has been married for some time to Davan, a nice girl from another village in the Western Federation. She is, perhaps understandably, a little suspicious of me at first, but after their first three children return to the All Life within days of their birth, she and I become quite close. Their next two children, both boys, will stay in this world. I become close to them too, and will be closer still to their children.

So when I tell Karel that it is at last time to visit the Traveller, I do so with a little trepidation, wondering if he is now too old to make the journey. His all-too-rare smile still has the same charm that it always had, mainly because although by now he has lost most of his hair, he has kept nearly all his teeth, and he's still sprightly for someone of his age. But he has grown used to the idea that his hunting days on the Sea of Grass are very far behind him, this being the main reason he allowed himself to be appointed Senior Councillor of the Western Federation and, as such, a Member of the Supreme Council.

However, Karel accepts my announcement without demur. He duly informs his startled fellow council members that he is leaving to seek the advice of the Traveller on the meaning of the sign apparently given to us so many years earlier, in the form of the cut wheat bound up in Frey's dead hand. They ask him precisely where he expects to find the Traveller.

This is a reasonable question: years earlier, the Sea of Grass had reached Her solitary house, which, unprotected by the trees, is now a ruin. But Karel has an answer to this, one with which I have supplied him. We need the Traveller's advice on the significance of the wheat found in Frey's hand, he explains. If he goes to where that wheat grows on the Sea of Grass, he will surely find the

Traveller there. No one can argue with this, so a week or so later, Karel and I set off.

*

I've never really understood how I could have such a vivid memory of that first journey across the Sea of Grass when I was Maya, but have next to no memory of making almost the same journey with Karel after I had become Arlen. But then I suppose so much had changed—as I said just now, the continued spread of the Sea of Grass had by this time effectively wiped out the Northern Federation, and even our village in the Western Federation is now less than two days from its edge—and, of course, I had become a different person. Whatever the explanation, in what seems to be an absurdly short time, I am again looking at the stick-like shapes about a few hundred paces ahead of me.

It is the same old wheat gathering camp that we visited so many years before. For a long time, all I can do is stand staring at it, remembering all that has happened since last we were here. I look around, half expecting to see Gorn standing there with the customary sneer on his face or Rona examining one of the nearby clumps of wheat. But all I see is Karel. I point to the wheat. He looks at it obediently, and I wait for the look of comprehension to appear on his face. Finally, it does, and he nods slowly.

"That time we were here before. All those years ago. You were trying to tell me something about the wheat. You wondered why that old, curved knife of mine was made to cut wheat or uproot it when we weren't doing either but picking it. I didn't understand, but you promised me that it would become clear to me later."

He unties his curved knife from his belt and looks at it. Then he laughs. "This is later, I suppose."

"Yes. Quite a bit later than I first envisaged. I'm sorry."

He shakes his head. "It doesn't matter."

Karel tucks the curved knife back into his belt, then walks over to the wheat and starts examining the ripe ears. Then he picks one and looks closely at it. He picks a second, then a third. He gives a little grunt. "It's the same kind that Frey had in her hand after she went with the White Plague. The kind that only grows here, that waits to be picked." He looks back at me. "What do you want me to do?"

"I want you to gather this wheat. Not by picking it, but by cutting it at the base of the stalks with your curved knife. I know you won't be able to take a lot back with you, but you won't need much. You just need enough to show everyone how this wheat contains a kind that is different, a kind that will wait for you to come and take it. You will explain how this gives people the power to control it. You will explain this to everyone in our village and to as many as you can in the rest of the Federation. And you will tell the Traders to carry word of it throughout the other Federations. Doing this will change all your lives forever."

Karel frowns. "But what about asking the Traveller's advice about all this? Isn't that the reason we've come here?" But as he waits for me to answer, his old, lined face suddenly goes slack with surprise, and his mouth falls open. He tries to speak, but it takes him two or three attempts before any actual words come out. "The Traveller's right here, isn't She?" he says finally. "All this time. All these years we've been together, and I never knew. I never guessed." He shakes his head slowly. "It's so clear to me now. I don't know how I could have been so stupid."

I put my hand on his shoulder. "You're being a little hard on yourself. I didn't really know either. Not until now."

He puts his hand over mine and squeezes it. Then after a few moments, he straightens slightly, steps away from me and turns back to the wheat.

"This thing you want me to do. You do realise that it will take me the rest of the time I have? And that that isn't long?"

"Yes, I do. In fact, it will take the entire lifetimes of your sons and your grandchildren as well. Because this is the single most important thing that each of you will ever do."

Karel frowns. "What do you mean?" he asks, suddenly sounding alarmed. "Won't You be with me?"

Explaining to Karel what I needed to do next meant telling him that he and I would never see one another again, and, silly as it may sound now, I suddenly realised how unprepared for this I was. But as I looked away from him, wondering what to say, something in the old camp caught my eye. It seemed that it wasn't deserted after all, but that one of the structures was, in fact, a very small but quite intact tent, a wisp of smoke curling out the top. I remember turning back to Karel to ask him if he had seen it as well. But by then, Karel had been gone for a very long time.

I walk to the tent, pull back the deerskin flap and step inside. It is very dark, the only source of light being a small fire. The moment I see it, I become completely disoriented: I have stepped inside a tent barely large enough for two people, but the fire inside it is at least twenty paces away from me. I look around and immediately become aware not just of spaciousness, but spaciousness of a kind wholly new to me. I am not standing in a tent at all but in some sort of house, although one unlike any I have ever seen before.

As my eyes grow used to the dim light, I can just about make out a figure on the far side of the small fire. However, I can't tell if it's a man or a woman, not just because he or she is seated, but because what they are sitting on is itself quite unlike any other piece of furniture I've ever seen. It is tall and slender, making the figure seated on it adopt an oddly erect posture, and there are narrow supports rising from either side of the actual seat on which the figure has placed their forearms.

Then I notice that this strange seat is itself placed on some kind of low platform, comprised of large stones. Each stone appears to have been shaped into regular blocks, as though they were made of wood rather than stone, then fitted together so closely that it would be hard to insert an arrowhead between them. These blocks are in turn placed upon a smooth floor of some pale-coloured material that it takes me a few moments more to recognize as burnt lime, the kind that in my village we used to line the walls of the grain silos.

I look up, trying to tell what kind of space this is. I can tell that there must be a roof I realise that there must be a roof because I can see nothing of the sky, but it is so far above me that it is completely lost in darkness and smoke from the fire in the middle of the floor near the stone platform. Then I forget about the roof because in looking up and then around, I am suddenly confronted with the standing stone on my left. It is like the stones making up the platform on which the still-silent figure is sitting, in that it has been carved into a regular shape as though made of mere wood or antler. But unlike the stones comprising the platform, this standing stone is enormous, easily four times the height of the tallest man. Then something on its face seems to move, and I see the lion, rearing up on its hind legs and lashing out with its left paw, teeth exposed in a fearsome snarl. It is very skilfully carved, but the reason I find it so difficult to take my eyes from it is that it reminds me of some other carvings from a very distant time. I am still trying to remember which, when the seated figure finally speaks.

"Hello, Arlen. I've been waiting for you."

On hearing the familiar voice, the panic I've been quietly trying to control vanishes. I step over to the fire so that I can face the figure directly.

Maya.

The light from the fire is poor, but somehow, I can see that her hair is longer and a lot wilder than I remember and is now liberally streaked with grey. But aside from that, and the fact that she is a grown woman whereas when I last saw her, she was a girl, she is little changed. Watching me studying her, Maya smiles almost apologetically.

"As you can see, there's only the one seat in here. You're welcome to it, but to be honest, I wouldn't recommend it." She looks awkwardly down at the strange thing she's sitting on. "It's unbelievably uncomfortable, which is remarkable, given how much work must have gone into making it."

"It was you," I finally manage to say. "All the time. You were the Traveller. You were the voice."

She looks up at me and holds my gaze for a long time before looking down into the tiny fire.

"Well, perhaps I was once," she replies with a sigh. "Although that depends on who you mean. We were all very different then. I did try to tell you."

I look around again at our strange surroundings.

"What is this place?"

"I suppose that's for you to decide. I've never been here before either. And before you ask, I don't know how I got here now."

I know that my next question is somewhat crass, but I can't help asking it. "Who exactly are you?"

She shrugs. "I am who I am." She begins to laugh at the look I give her, but then stops herself. "I'm sorry. That was a bit self-indulgent, wasn't it? But a simple question doesn't imply a simple answer."

"Oh, please don't apologise," I can't help snapping back. "You never gave me any kind of answer when you were the voice. And no one has ever had a proper answer from the Traveller on anything. Why should it be any different now?"

Maya frowns. "What do you mean, a proper answer?"

I step closer to her. "You know perfectly well what I mean. An answer that wasn't incomplete. One that explained the consequences of what you told us to do."

Maya looks at me evenly. Suddenly, she smiles. "You were afraid I'd be old, weren't you?"

"Yes."

Her smile fades. "Whereas I'm afraid that you won't know me."

I step even closer to her, close enough for me to reach up and touch the freckles across her nose, the small pale birthmark near her jawline, the small scar on her cheek, the mole on her chin. Her yellow-flecked, pale brown eyes are on mine as I touch her face, and I can see the apprehension in them. I lower my hand.

"You're right to be afraid," I say. "Because now I realise that I never knew you at all."

Maya returns my gaze but does not reply.

"I suppose you're going to tell me how sorry you are that it all had to be like this," I go on, surprised at the bitterness in my voice.

At this, Maya looks genuinely taken aback. "No. We may not have seen each other in a long time, but surely you know me better than that. Surely you know I'd never say anything so pointless."

She looks at me with renewed curiosity. This time, it is I who cannot hold her gaze, and I drop my eyes.

"I see," she says after a few moments. She sighs. "Look, there's no point in you pretending that any of this comes as a shock. You've known for a long time. I know how hard you've pretended to yourself that you haven't, but you have."

"Known what?" I retort. "That I'm the reason that all those people were murdered?"

"Yes," says Maya, with another sigh. "Amongst other things."

I look down again into the tiny fire. I have wanted to hear her voice for so long, and now that I am hearing it, I find it almost too difficult to bear. "Why do you want to talk about this now? How is it going to help? Are you seriously suggesting that there's any kind of excuse for what was done? For what we did? Because there isn't."

Maya shakes her head.

"No. I know there isn't. But I don't want to talk about this right now. Because right now, it doesn't matter. It isn't why you and I are here."

For a moment, I cannot believe what she's just said.

"How dare you say that?" I finally manage to whisper. "It matters."

I stare at her, willing her to meet my gaze. When finally she does, she looks stricken. Then she closes her eyes, and her shoulders droop. "You don't understand, do you? I don't know why, but all this time, I was so certain that you would. I'm not talking about all the ones who died. I'm not saying their deaths don't matter. How can I, of all people, say that? I don't need to remind you how we have felt every last bit of their terror, their pain, their grief, their rage, their—" She pauses, eyes closed. "Their infinite sense of unjust loss," she continues after a few moments. "It has been a part of me ever since. So much so that sometimes it feels as though that is now all I am. All that I ever will be." She opens her eyes again. "I've tried so often to tell myself that it would have happened anyway. That it always does in one way or another. Or at one time or another. Whenever there are too many people and not enough of everything else. Or whenever there is enough for everyone, but people aren't willing to share it."

"And do you find that that helps you? Because it isn't helping me. Not one little bit."

Maya shakes her head.

"Of course not. But then, why should it? The fact is, it was done by those who felt they had our encouragement. Our approval. But that is precisely what you need to understand now. It doesn't matter if you hate me or Serris or Frey or Bran for doing what we did. All that matters now is that you understand what you are. What we are."

Maya—I am having great difficulty seeing her as the Traveller—looks at me for a long time, then back at the fire. She prods at it with her foot and the flame jumps, lighting up her face.

"Don't you see?" She continues, gazing down into the flames. "That this is the only way this can work? They needed our help to survive before, and now they need our help again. But they can only accept it if they can believe that whatever they do, good or bad, you and I are responsible, and not them."

Maya looks up at me imploringly, as though willing me to understand. I am not in the mood to try.

"What are you talking about? We are responsible. The reason that my—our—parents did what they did was because we made them believe it was what we wanted. You told them that I—that we—had to be protected, no matter what. When we told them that, we knew perfectly well how they would understand it, what they would take it to mean. And when they tried to find some other way, any other way, we gave them absolutely no help at all. We began all this, not them. We set it all in motion. Serris was right when she told me about this all those years ago. She, Bran, Frey, all of them. They were just tools. No, weapons. Weapons that were wielded by us. Weapons that we used to murder hundreds of people. We have no right to try to put any of the responsibility onto them. Or onto anyone but ourselves."

There is a long silence.

When Maya finally speaks again, her voice sounds even more hoarse than my own, so hoarse that it is almost a whisper.

"Yes. Everything you say is true. And that's something else you need to understand. We may never be forgiven for it."

Her calmness makes me so furious that I want to say

something to hurt her, to make her feel something of my pain and anger.

"What is this, self-pity?" I ask, in the cruellest tone I can manage. "Please, spare me that. It really is the least you can do."

Maya leans forward in her strange seat, staring at me. "You still don't see it, do you?"

She shakes her head then takes a deep breath.

"You're right. You, we, made our parents believe that we wanted them to murder all those people because it was the only way to avoid everyone starving to death. But that is exactly what has enabled you now to make them understand why the wheat on the Sea of Grass is so special. How they will actually be able to control its very production. How that will mean that they don't have to wait for the next danger to arise but can actually prevent it arising in the first place. How they can at last break the circle."

She reaches her arms out towards me.

"Can you really not see that this is only possible because of the agreement we have made with them? The bargain by which we can help them, and in return, they can believe that we are responsible for everything that happens as a result? And that now, there's no going back on it? Because there isn't. From now on, whatever they do, they will tell themselves that it's what you want, that it is your will. With that belief, they will be able to do truly wonderful things. But—"

Maya stops, staring intently into my eyes, wanting me to finish her sentence, which I do.

"—they will also be able to do some truly terrible things."

She nods emphatically. "Yes. And not only that. Because of their belief that they are doing your will, they will demand, insist, on your forgiveness for all those terrible things. And you will have no choice but to forgive them. Because that is what you will have made them believe."

It is the grief in her eyes that finally makes me understand.

"But there may never be any forgiveness for me," I whisper.

Maya is silent for a long time, tears now running down her face. But then she wipes them away with a decisive gesture. "Who knows? One day, there may be. Perhaps from those from whom you least expect it."

I don't know why I say what I say next.

"Tell me one thing first. You say that if those people hadn't been killed, we would all die. But so what if we do? Why shouldn't we all die? Would it be so awful if we all returned to the All Life?"

Maya sits back in her strange chair, looking at me in astonishment. "If we all return to the All Life?" she repeats. Then she looks away, shaking her head again.

"Oh dear." She sighs. "It never occurred to me that you hadn't understood that either."

Then she looks back at me, and when she speaks, it is as though to a small child.

"The All Life is where we are now. Where all of us have always been. It's just as we were always told: We are the All Life, and the All Life is us. The question isn't whether we all die and return to the All Life. It's whether we all stay as part of the All Life. Living or dead."

*

I remember suddenly feeling so tired that I had to sit down on the low platform made of the fitted stone blocks and that I could not stop myself from closing my eyes. I don't remember anything else from this time, the time when I first saw what would become the first of my many new homes. But I do remember what happened after I found myself once again alone in my house which, uniquely, was never part of any village but which stood by itself, a long way to the north, half a day from what used to be the most northerly village of the Northern Federation.

*

Although I never got to say goodbye to him, Karel did return to our village, where he began the slow process of explaining what the Traveller had revealed to him concerning the wheat he had

179

brought back. As he had already guessed, it would take him the rest of the time he had left in his world and that of his sons and his grandchildren. However, the necessary change would only come through actions, not words, and they would take much longer.

The first step is persuading some of the wheat to leave its home and make a new one amongst the villages, which means first determining what kind of soil is most like that in which it grows on the Sea of Grass. It turns out that the soil of the northerly parts of the Western Federation itself is ideal, with a fair amount of clay, not too sour yet not too chalky. This is fortunate in the short term, although it is going to give rise to serious difficulties later.

The next step is establishing the best way of encouraging the wheat to germinate in this soil, whether by scattering it on the ground or by digging small holes in it and placing the seed pods inside. In the end, it seems that scattering it on lightly broken ground then covering it with a small amount of soil yields the best results. At about the same time, all the nearby flowers, shrubs and creepers, some of which seem really to resent the newcomer, have to be dissuaded from strangling it as it grows. But grow it does, and when it ripens, about one-fifth of it has seed pods that do not split and which will therefore wait to be gathered.

For the first few generations, attempting to make the wheat grow in the villages of the Western Federation on this constant trial and error basis, difficult and demanding as it is, remains a relatively marginal activity. People go on gathering roots, nuts, berries and fruits, as they always have. They continue to fish, not just with fish traps, but in time with large willow nets that can span Verba's tributaries, one edge suspended from the surface, the other weighted with stones securing it to the bottom. People still hunt, occasionally amongst the trees but mostly now on the Sea of Grass, as it has continued to expand. In due course, they become quite proficient at this, and in so doing develop a good working relationship with the animals there, particularly the horses.

Yet little by little—so slowly, in fact, that it is not really perceptible in the span of one life spent in this world—everyone comes to depend more and more on the wheat they are growing, until only five or so generations after Karel first returned from the Sea of Grass with the wheat he had cut there, the villages of the Western Federation have more food than they need to prevent them from going hungry. Yet there is no jubilation or even any sense of relief. Because by this time, it has become clear that one set of problems has merely been exchanged for another.

*

Up to this point, land is simply the particular manifestation in this world of the part of the All Life on and in which most things necessary to stay in this world are found, such as animals hunted and trapped for food and clothing, nuts, seeds, fruits, roots, shrubs and flowers picked for food and medicines, or heather or nettles or timber taken to make rope, goat and sheep pens, or houses.

The Law dictates where a village might go to find all these things, how much of them may be taken and how any surplus is to be shared, along with dozens of other details. But it has never recognized the idea that the land itself—the actual ground in and on which all these things may be found—is capable of being owned in the same way as a knife, a fire kit or a piece of jewellery is owned, because up until this point, such an idea would have been meaningless.

Yet suddenly, the people in the villages trying to make the wheat grow begin to feel that somehow, they do indeed own the land on which it is growing. And now, the Western Federation has, from this land, produced more food than it needs, when the villages of the other two Federations are hungry because they cannot yet do so. A serious problem is developing, and for the first time in its existence, the Law cannot solve it.

In a series of increasingly tense discussions, the Councils of the Southern and Eastern Federations protest that it is not their fault that the Traveller chose to reveal the secrets of this new food source to a man from the Western Federation, or that the ground in which their own villages are located does not favour the growing wheat nearly so well as the ground on which the villages of the

Western Federation stand. The Council of the Western Federation replies that it is only because of the hard work of their villages in making the ground suitable for growing wheat when previously it was not, that there is any food surplus at all.

In an attempt at compromise, the Council of the Western Federation proposes that the surplus will be shared, provided that the Eastern and Southern Federations give an immediate guarantee that any future food surplus they produce will be shared. But they refuse, complaining that this is effectively coercion. The deadlock is referred to the Supreme Council, but the Supreme Council cannot break it because the Council of the Western Federation, knowing that the members of the Supreme Council will simply divide along Federation lines, makes it known in advance that it will resist the imposition of any solution, whether by the Supreme Council or any of the Law Sayers.

The tension between the Federations then rises still further due to another, equally unforeseen consequence of the reliance on the new food source. The villages in the Western Federation, who have put so much time and effort into growing the wheat on the land in which they are located, now cannot leave that land. At the same time, each house in each of those villages holds the remains of members of those families who have left this world for the All Life, precisely so that they can move with their families, even if in fact those families may not move for many generations. Once it is obvious that these families will never move again, it becomes equally obvious that these particular family members want a permanent home of their own, and they make it clear to their relatives that until this is provided, they will be deeply unhappy.

It is at this point that some Federation Councillor somewhere suggests doing something that has not been done for a very long time: seeking the advice of the Traveller. Yet even that is not as straightforward as it once was. This is less to do with so many generations having passed since Karel returned to our village from the Sea of Grass with My advice about the wheat, and more to do with the novel way in which Karel had sought My advice in the first place.

Whenever My advice had been required before, a messenger had gone to the house that stood by itself a long way to the north, half a day from what used to be the most northerly village of the Northern Federation. But as I explained a little while ago, Karel wasn't able to do that, as this house had by then become a ruin, and had instead told everyone that the Traveller had come to him, visiting him as he camped by a wheat patch on the Sea of Grass. So once again, seeking the advice of the Traveller means first having to ascertain where the Traveller might be found, but this time without any clues.

The answer of the Council of the Western Federation to this conundrum is to build Me a new house, then wait for me to go and live in it so that I can be found there.

You might consider this answer naïve, if not a little presumptuous. I know I did. So perhaps you can imagine my surprise when it turned out to be correct.

*

This naivety was perhaps most apparent in My new house being rebuilt in exactly the same location and of more or less the same materials, despite the fact that it was exposure to the incessant wind and drenching rain of the Sea of Grass that had destroyed the original. And yet, as it turned out, that too served a useful purpose.

I don't now remember much about the first delegation that found me in this rebuilt house, except that it was from the Western Federation. I therefore can't remember when I first realised that there might be one solution to the two apparently quite separate problems created by the increasing dependence on wheat.

I do recall telling this delegation that only part of that single solution lay here, in this time, and that the other part lay elsewhere, in another time, and that I therefore had no choice but to Travel to this other time to find it. I also told them that this other time would seem to them to be very distant, so that for Me to Travel there would seem to them to take many hundreds of generations. But, I said, the fact that they had built me a new house had shown how I could at the same time both Travel to this distant time and yet remain amongst them in a way I had never done before.

I was, I said, very grateful for my new house. However, I explained, it could not be expected to survive long. The change in circumstances—being exposed on the Sea of Grass, whereas once the house had been sheltered by the trees—meant that it was not suitable for the purpose it was now expected to fulfil. And that, I said, was true of their own houses, at least as regards those with whom they shared them, the family members whose remains they had brought back from their respective Stations to be buried beneath their floors.

I also told this delegation that it was for the Western Federation to address these problems. The food surplus it had created had, I said, given it unprecedented power, but that with power came responsibility. The Western Federation therefore had to build another new house, one that was fit for a new purpose and therefore unlike any other house built before.

This, I told them, would be a house for every single village in all three Federations. And it would be a house not merely for the remains of their relatives but also for Me so that I could dwell amongst everyone—those still confined to this world and those who were not. I would show them how to make this house out of stone, as the houses in which the Lost Ones dwelt were of stone. Because, I said, it was to the Lost Ones in their distant time to whom I now had to travel to find the rest of the solution, even as I continue to dwell amongst the people of the delegation's time.

The delegation wasn't at all happy with any of this.

When the shock of what I had said began to wear off, the objections began.

Some objected that the Western Federation simply did not have the labour force necessary to build a house large enough to serve as a Station for the villages of all three Federations, whether or not it was also a house for Me. So I had to explain that they could obtain the labour of the villages in the other two Federations because they would have no choice but to trade this labour for a share both of the existing surplus food and of all future surpluses.

Then some objected that demanding labour in exchange for food was surely against the Law. So I had to remind them that they could no longer rely on the Law, as that had been shown incapable of dealing with the present situation.

There were other objections, all of them just as understandable. Yet none of them had anything to do with the real reason for the delegates' deep unhappiness with what I had said. So I also told them that I understood this. I said that I knew they feared any contact with the Lost Ones, even contact through Myself: and that, even more than that, they feared emulating the Lost Ones by making a house built entirely of stone.

So I told them that I was not asking the villages of the Western Federation to emulate the Lost Ones, but to help them. And I told the delegates that if everyone could work together in a way they had never done before, for a new common purpose, they could change their lives forever. But, I said, this would not be enough if all people, including the Lost Ones, were to survive. That could only be accomplished if the people of this time understood how the Lost Ones went so very wrong and if the Lost Ones themselves understood that they were not in fact truly Lost.

This, I told the delegation, was why the rest of the solution to their problems lay in the distant time of the Lost Ones and therefore why I had to Travel there. For now, I said, the delegation had to take back My advice to the villages of the Western Federation, and they had to act upon it. For by doing so, they would continue what they had in fact already started: the process of changing the world.

*

Well, that's what I said.

You hardly need me to tell you that hunger did not disappear. Yet at least it didn't drive people from the world completely as it had threatened to do when I was a child. And within only a

185

few years of that delegation's visit, the Western Federation did indeed organize themselves and many others from the Eastern and Southern Federations sufficiently to build a large house, made almost entirely of stone.

Again there was a great deal of trial and error, although significantly less than that involved in making the wheat grow. It didn't take long to work out that finding the right kind of stone, pounding lumps of it into the right shapes and fitting them together, wasn't so very different from doing the same with wood and antler, except, of course, that it took far longer and needed many more people to do the heavy lifting.

In building this new kind of house, the villages of the Western Federation, together with the villages of the Southern and Eastern Federations who had indeed traded their labour for food, began to develop a new sense of themselves and their potential, not just as individuals, but collectively. This bound all three Federations more closely together than ever before. So did the fact that this new house of stone had ample room for all that remained in this world of the people from all three Federations who were no longer confined to it. They could stay there in their comfortable and very grand new surroundings for as long as their families wished them to, which seemed to solve the problem that had been the cause of so much unhappiness.

As well as all this, people realised that having made one kind of stone building that was capable of withstanding the wind and rains of the Sea of Grass, they could make another. New, far stronger and more durable homes for people still confined to this world could now be built on the Sea of Grass. Soon, a dozen villages of largely stone houses were spread across it, the existing trading networks spreading with them, comprising a new, second Northern Federation. Then this new Northern Federation built another large stone house in which, as I had said so long before I would, I lived, just as I lived in the first such house built by the Western Federation.

I don't want to give you the impression that all this happened without any problems. There were plenty, but I don't propose to tell you about all of them, because the point I really want to make is that generally, this time was peaceful. And compared to how things had been when I was growing up, they were even prosperous.

Of course, things didn't stay like that for very long.

*

Within a few more generations, the four Federations coalesced into one. But this new, single Federation differed in one important respect from its older, constituent parts. For all their squabbles, resentments and rivalries, each one of those earlier Federations had defined themselves by reference to the others, and since all were essentially the same, no one Federation could ever really feel superior to another. Yet many people within this new Federation felt very superior indeed to the new people with whom, through the extended trading networks, they were now coming into contact. None of these people—from those in the fertile lands nestling improbably in the deserts in the south, to the nomads in the forests of the northwest which the Sea of Grass had never reached—could grow their own food, or build houses of stone, or had a legal system anywhere near as sophisticated as that of the Federation. However, whilst despising them for what they lacked, the people in the ever-growing villages of the Federation coveted what they did have: a seemingly endless supply of land on which wheat could be grown, land which was not, as so much of the Federation's own land now was, overcrowded, stinking and becoming riddled with disease. It was therefore only a matter of time before someone on the Council of the Federation remembered how, so many generations earlier, competition for resource—previously, food, but now land on which food could be grown—could be reduced by the expedient of organized mass murder.

But this time, the perpetrators did not see their victims as more or less identical to themselves but as vastly inferior. This made the steps first to the threat, then to the use of violence as a means of acquiring the precious land so much shorter and easier, and the violence in question was on a scale that made the Massacres from my childhood look almost insignificant. And nearly all those who planned and inflicted this violence did so in the confident belief that they had My full support.

I wish I could tell you that all this was somehow part of My plan and that, terrible as it was, there was some kind of higher purpose to it. But I can't. If I'm honest, I don't remember if I even foresaw it, although if I did, I doubt I would have changed My plan, because I could not see any other way of doing what I needed to do.

I'm sorry if that disappoints you. But I did tell you when we began that I'm not perfect.

*

I'm close to finishing this story of mine, as the point at which people start using organized violence against one another to acquire and then retain land is probably the one at which things will become depressingly familiar to you. But I do want to tell you about one visit I received, very soon after the second stone house had been built for me by the Northern Federation and when I was still getting used to them.

I can't remember what name I was known by then, although that hardly matters: there have been so many names now, and I answer to them all. I do remember opening my eyes and experiencing that sense of complete bewilderment one has on waking from a deep sleep of vivid dreaming. I place my hands down onto whatever it is I am sitting on, and my bewilderment turns to mild panic. I can feel that it is wood, but the way it moves slightly as I shift in it tells me that it isn't a carved block, but something made of various separate parts somehow fitted together. I look down and see that whatever I am seated on is itself on some kind of low platform, comprised of large stones shaped into regular blocks and then fitted together and placed on a smooth burnt lime floor.

I can make this out from the light of a small fire in a square hearth, itself made of smaller, shaped stone blocks. I look around.

In the dim light, I can just about make out a curving wall that seems to go all around me, creating a roughly circular area about thirty paces in diameter. That, and the strange sound my breathing is making, tells me that this is some kind of enclosed, but very large, space. And only then do I notice the young man standing on the far side of the fire, so close to me that I wonder how he could have arrived there without my seeing him.

The young man is staring at me intently. This is surprising and makes me feel a little shy, as it is a long time since anyone has looked at me so directly. His expression is also surprising. He looks almost nonplussed, as though I am the very last person he was expecting to see.

"It's funny, isn't it? Funny how a place can be strange yet familiar at the same time."

The young man frowns and seems to ponder my somewhat banal comment as though it were of the greatest significance.

"I do not know," he says finally. He speaks slowly, seeming to choose his words with great care as though he is uncertain, although whether of himself or of me, I can't tell.

We look at one another for several long and rather awkward moments, and I begin to sense that he expects me to recognize him. I don't, yet somehow, he seems familiar. Finally, I speak just to break the silence.

"I don't mean to be rude or anything," I say in what I hope is a polite tone. "But do I know you? I do, don't I?"

Again, this simple question seems to leave the young man quite dumbfounded. "I don't know," he replies finally. Then he shrugs. "I'm just a man."

I am wondering what to say in answer to this when memory comes flooding back with such force that I feel as though I am going to faint. I half expect the young man to jump forwards and catch me, but he remains still, his face impassive.

"You'll have to excuse me. I ought to introduce myself. But introducing oneself usually means first explaining who one is. And it's been so long since I've been able to do that."

There is a long pause in which the young man again seems

to be weighing up my words with far more deliberation than they deserve.

"Perhaps that does not matter," he says tentatively. "Since You came to live amongst us, we have been looking for You harder than ever. Perhaps we have all been looking so hard that we have begun to lose sight of You."

"We?" I ask him quickly. He looks at me blankly.

"You said, We have all been looking for You. Are there more of you, then?"

But again, the young man doesn't answer. He is clearly terribly confused—however he may have anticipated this conversation going, it was obviously nothing like this—and his confusion is confusing me. I want more than ever to ask him exactly who he is, but somehow, I know that it will do no good. So I rephrase the question.

"Who are the other people who come here? Are they people like you?"

"People like me?" replies the young man finally, still sounding surprised, but rather less so this time. "Well, yes, I suppose so. But right now, it's just—" He pauses again.

"Just us," he finishes.

I cannot resist the opportunity presented by his apologetic tone.

"And who exactly are we?"

"Who exactly are we?" the young man repeats. He frowns again. "I can't really speak for anyone else," he continues after a few moments. "As for me, well, as I said just now, I'm just a man. Whereas you—"

He stops abruptly and seems at a loss as to how to carry on.

"Whereas I?" I prompt him.

The young man does not say anything but merely looks at me as though waiting for me to complete his sentence. Clearly, I will have to be more direct.

"Who do people say that I am?"

I am expecting the young man to look surprised, but instead, his expression has turned to that of someone who has to give some distressing news that he would really rather not give. He looks down at the smooth, lime covered floor and sighs.

"A very long time ago," he says, "it was said that You were the one who could pass between worlds. That You could travel between our world, the world that we see around us, and all other worlds. And that these other worlds included a world in which all the animals and all the people who ever were, and who would ever be, lived as a single spirit. It was said that by travelling between worlds in this way, You could learn all that people here needed to know so that they might carry on living in this world. Things such as how to create and care for fire, how to make proper houses and clothing that would protect us, how to find the food we needed, and even how to make proper homes for those of us who are dead." He pauses, looking uncertain.

"Go on," I say.

"But then the world began to get colder. The Sea of Grass began to push back the trees, which up until then had been the source of all our food. So we began to grow hungry until the hunger made us kill one another. But then You showed us that we ourselves were capable of changing the world. You showed us how we could make wheat grow and how we could make a proper place for those of us who are dead, a place that was also a house in which You would stay, to live amongst us."

He gestures around with one arm.

"So we built such a place, and then another. And in doing so, we began to abandon our old ways, as You knew we would. But although we have all this new knowledge, we do not yet have the wisdom that should go with it. So we had no understanding of what abandoning our old ways would mean. No knowledge of the terrible price that would have to be paid."

The young man looks at me again, and for the first time, there seems to be something accusing in his gaze.

"Some say that these are things You could never have intended." He stops abruptly and looks away, shaking his head.

"Forgive me," he says quietly. "I did not mean to sound as if I were judging in any way. It is not for me to do so."

My short peal of laughter is followed by another and even more awkward silence.

"I'm sorry," I say at last. "That must have seemed very rude. But I wasn't laughing at you. I was just surprised. Surprised that you feel it's not your place to judge Me, when it so clearly is. After all, that is part of the reason that you and all the others come to see Me, isn't it?"

The young man stands silent, head bowed.

"It's all right," I go on. "I know it is. But in judging Me, you must never believe that I do not know death. I know it better than anyone. If I had not lived and died so many times, I could never have understood just what the cost would be, the price to which you just referred. The price that this place and all the other places like it yet to be built represents. But there was simply no other way."

"No other way to do what?"

I don't know why I choose this time to be so honest.

"To speak to the Lost Ones."

At this, the young man frowns again, but this time in puzzlement, his head cocked on one side. It has not occurred to me that he may not recognize the phrase.

"I have to speak to them," I go on. "Because they too have knowledge without wisdom. As you do. As do I."

"You?" he whispers. His mouth falls open in surprise. Even in that one short word, his utter incredulity is clear, and I cannot help smiling again.

"Oh yes. It's something that someone once tried to tell me, in a very different time, about being a child no longer. Back then, I assumed She meant other people. Now I know She meant Me."

I expect the young man to look more confused than ever. But in fact, he is nodding slowly.

"And this is what connects us? The people of my time, these Lost Ones, and You? We all have knowledge without wisdom?"

"Yes. So perhaps you understand why I had to try to speak to them, as well as to you."

He notices my sudden hesitation.

"But there is something else?"

Instead of replying, and rather to my surprise, I find myself reaching my hands out to him. He steps closer to me to take both of them in his.

"There is something else about these Lost Ones that means You must keep trying to speak with them?" he asks.

I look at my tiny, wizened hands nestling in his large, strong, young ones.

"Yes." Suddenly my voice is so weak and hoarse I can barely whisper. "I must speak to them, because it is only to them that I can confess what I have done. And if I do not confess, I can never be forgiven." I blink and see large tears fall and land with tiny splashes onto the young man's hands as they hold mine. He is silent for several moments.

"I understand," he says at last. "You cannot seek our forgiveness because you cannot confess to us what You have done. And You cannot do that because it is we whom You first made do such terrible things. You and we are complicit. So the only people from whom you may seek forgiveness are these Lost Ones. Having become Lost to You, You are not as responsible for them as You are for us. Not complicit with them as You are complicit with us."

He releases my hands and stands back, looking around himself again, but now as though he is seeing this place for the first time.

"Of course," he says softly. "That is the other reason You wanted us to make places like this. Perhaps the most important reason of all. You knew that in another time, these Lost Ones would discover them, or what in their time, what remains of them. You knew that in finding them and then in trying to understand their purpose, the Lost Ones will begin to understand You a little better and might one day understand how You helped stop us from vanishing from the world, and the terrible price that had to be paid for doing so. If they do, You can make your confession to them. And perhaps they might forgive You."

"Yes. But I am not hopeful."

The young man looks at me. For a moment, his face is quite

expressionless. Then he smiles broadly. "Oh, I don't know," he says, his tone suddenly light and casual. "They may be Lost to You and You to them, but they're still people. And if people understood You once, they can understand You again. If they do, they might forgive You. And if that happens, they may not be the Lost Ones after all."

It was already late when I began telling you this story. Now, I can just about see the top edge of the sun above the western hills, which means that within an hour, it will be quite dark.

I like coming back to this place. There are so many like it, but none are quite the same. Perhaps that's why I have such a strong attachment to it, or perhaps it's because so many people from this time see it as the place where this story really began, although in many ways, it actually marks the end of it. Whatever the reason, I feel particularly at home here.

The last of the day's many tourists have already been gently ushered back towards the main site entrance by their guides and onto their enormous, air-conditioned coaches which will carry them back to their hotels in the town, about an hour away. Taner and Asil, the security team, are making their final round of the site, locking all the gates in the three-metre-high wire fence enclosing it. Taner is looking forward to getting home to see his wife and their new baby daughter, hoping that little Elif will still be awake. He tells me that Elif is particularly precious because she will bring him and his wife Hira closer together again. He is in fact quite mistaken about this: he and Hira have drifted apart because she is quite simply bored with him and with their marriage, and Elif's arrival will not change this. However, Hira has told me that she will not leave Taner, because she is afraid of being on her own more than she is afraid of a life of boredom with him.

Taner is so preoccupied that he is only half-listening to Asil as he chatters away to him. Asil himself is well aware of this, but he keeps talking anyway. Most people like Asil well enough, but they find him rather trivial. I have told him that this is mainly due to his tendency to prattle, so that doing so to try and get people to take him seriously is somewhat counterproductive. But even though Asil appreciates this, there are times when he can't help himself.

As Taner and Asil continue securing the site perimeter, the trio of archaeologists, having said goodnight to their small army of student volunteers a little while earlier, are packing up for the night. Birgitte, the dig director, and her deputy Jens are carefully covering up the current excavations, whilst their colleague Marius locks away the equipment and the precious Finds trays in the secure storage units. All three are used to the tourists being hugely impressed by the site itself and the standing stones in particular, but being disappointed by the relatively unspectacular nature of the recent finds. Birgitte tells me that this is worrying her more and more. The site admission fees and the profits from the visitor centre have become a major source of funding, so that if the number of tourists don't remain high, there may not be the money for another season's dig. This is certainly a concern, although it is not the real reason for her anxiety.

When Birgitte believes that Marius is safely out of sight, she turns to Jens and kisses him, and he responds with his usual passion. Both have told me that they have always known their relationship would be short, and that one day, Birgitte would have to return to her husband and Jens to his girlfriend, but I know that there is rather more to it than that. Jens is now in love with Birgitte but knows that she is not in love with him. Birgitte knows Jens knows this but has nonetheless become emotionally dependent on the intensity of Jens' feelings for her, and finds the prospect of being without them almost unbearable.

As for Marius, he has in fact known about the relationship between Birgitte and Jens more or less since it began. Yet although he sometimes finds their secretiveness a little irritating, he is too fond of them both actually to say anything and anyway, I know how preoccupied he is with money worries. His wife Sofie is pregnant with their first child, and he has yet to tell her that their financial situation has just taken a marked turn for the worse, mainly because of his online gambling habit.

Soon enough, Birgitte, Jens and Marius join Taner and Asil at the main site entrance. Having locked it, all five squeeze into Birgitte's old, dusty and dented car and head back to their homes and lodgings in the town. On their way there, they will of course chat away to one another, and once they have arrived, they will join all those others who are talking to others still, not just face to face but by smartphone, tablet and laptop, all chatting, confiding, confessing, complaining and gossiping. And all of them, every last one, is at the same time also talking to Me.

I have yet to solve the mystery of how so many millions of people in such immediate contact with one another nevertheless became so isolated that they grew to be the Lost Ones. It is the solution to this that I have Travelled so far to find. As I told you when we began, only someone who can be perceived by others can ever really be said to be alive, so forgiveness for Me depends not just on the Lost Ones feeling alive themselves, but feeling Me to be alive too: and still, so many do not.

Yet compared to how I felt when I spoke with that young man so long ago, when I was, I confess, at something of a low point, I have two reasons for feeling more optimistic. First, I have accepted that I will continue to reason my way ever closer to the solution I need, because I have no choice: we are all of us reasoning all the time as part of the endless process of creating our view of ourselves, of our world and who and what shares that world with us, each view unique to the mind that makes and re-makes it a million times every day, each view just as real and just as valid as any other. And second, nearly all the Lost Ones still include Me in their world—even though, as I say, so many of them don't realise it.

Sometimes, they do so by listening to stories like this one. And since that is what you have been good enough to do, I'd like to thank you. After all, telling you a story about Myself is a very intimate thing for both of us. I have to reveal Myself to you, but you have to let Me do so, which means you forming your own ideas of Me and the world I have told you about, ideas that will then become part of you. And I hope that in return, you may now feel you have the chance, if you want it, to be connected with so many other people, no matter where or when, in a way that you wcrc not before. Because whether I'm acknowledged, and whatever name I may be given, I cannot help but be with everyone.

https://noemathenovel.org/

A warm thank you to the following people, for making this book
possible

Dermitzel
Brak
Clacks
Jun Nozaki
Leon Sorensen
Agnes Merey
Gele Croom
Philip O'Loughlin
Steven Askew
Tucker Lieberman
Lachelle Seville

Your support is seen, felt, and appreciated so much. Because of
you, we can continue to put out the books we believe in.

If you'd like to support our press as well, you can find us over at
https://www.patreon.com/tRaumbooks.

You can also visit us online at
www.traumbooks.com